DOUBLE FEATURE

More twin-tastic fun
from Julia DeVillers
and Jennifer Roy

TRADING FACES

TAKE TWO

TIMES SQUARED

DOUBLE FEATURE

Julia DeVillers &
Jennifer Roy

m!x

ALADDIN M!X
NEW YORK   LONDON   TORONTO   SYDNEY   NEW DELHI

This book is a work of fiction. Any references to historical events, real people, or real places are used fictitiously. Other names, characters, places, and events are products of the author's imagination, and any resemblance to actual events or places or persons, living or dead, is entirely coincidental.

m!x

ALADDIN M!X

Simon & Schuster Children's Publishing Division

1230 Avenue of the Americas, New York, NY 10020

First Aladdin M!X edition December 2012

Copyright © 2012 by Julia DeVillers and Jennifer Roy

All rights reserved, including the right of reproduction in whole or in part in any form.

ALADDIN is a trademark of Simon & Schuster, Inc.,

and related logo is a registered trademark of Simon & Schuster, Inc.

ALADDIN M!X and related logo are registered trademarks of Simon & Schuster, Inc.

Also available in an Aladdin hardcover edition.

For information about special discounts for bulk purchases, please contact Simon & Schuster Special Sales at 1-866-506-1949 or business@simonandschuster.com.

The Simon & Schuster Speakers Bureau can bring authors to your live event.

For more information or to book an event contact the Simon & Schuster Speakers Bureau at 1-866-248-3049 or visit our website at www.simonspeakers.com.

Designed by Karin Paprocki

The text of this book was set in Granjon.

Manufactured in the United States of America 1112 OFF

2 4 6 8 10 9 7 5 3 1

The Library of Congress has cataloged the hardcover edition as follows:

DeVillers, Julia.

Double feature / Julia DeVillers, Jennifer Roy. — 1st Aladdin hardcover ed.

p. cm.

Summary: Twins Payton and Emma are off to Hollywood to star in a TV commercial, but nothing goes as planned, and it may take a twin switch or two to help things work out.

ISBN 978-1-4424-3402-8 (hc)

[1. Twins—Fiction. 2. Sisters—Fiction. 3. Television advertising—Fiction. 4. Television—Production and direction—Fiction. 5. Middle schools—Fiction. 6. Schools—Fiction. 7. Hollywood (Los Angeles, Calif.)—Fiction. 8. New York (N.Y.)—Fiction.] I. Roy, Jennifer Rozines, 1967– II. Title.

PZ7.D4974Dou 2012

[Fic]—dc23

2011038905

ISBN 978-1-4424-3403-5 (pbk)

ISBN 978-1-4424-3404-2 (eBook)

To Fiona Simpson,
who makes creating these books
double the fun

Payton

One

ON THE MORNING SCHOOL BUS

Sunglasses! Did I remember to bring sunglasses?

I opened my tote bag and scrounged around looking for them. I felt my brush and mirror. My cotton candy-flavored lip gloss. A chocolate-chip granola bar for after school.

And, phew, my sunglasses. I pulled out the pair of huge, round, white plastic sunglasses from my bag. I was going to need them after school for Drama Club. We were each supposed to bring a prop to fit the scene. My group was going to act out a scene on the beach, so I thought sunglasses would be perfect.

Plus they were cute. I slid my sunglasses on and

❖ 1 ❖

chilled, just looking out the window of the school bus. My sunglasses made it a little more challenging to see, but there really wasn't much to look at anyway: the usual houses, trees, people waiting for the bus. Definitely not as exciting as the bus I had been on earlier this week. That bus was a double-decker bus. In New York City!

Yes! I went to New York City with the Drama Club. We went to see our drama teacher's friend who was producing an almost-on-Broadway show. It was amazing! We went on the double-decker bus and toured the city. We also went to a giant toy store, stayed in a cool hotel room, and swam in the hotel pool.

And if that wasn't amazing enough . . .

We got to go onstage in the off-Broadway show! It was almost like we were Broadway stars!!!

Oh, and by we, I mean me and my sister, Emma. My twin sister. Emma and I look pretty much exactly alike.

I'm Payton, the twin who:

—is one inch taller

—has slightly greener eyes

—is dressed quite fashionably in her black T-shirt with the word "Broadway" across it in glitter, skinny jeans, and tall boots and is sitting in the back of the bus, where it's coolest to sit because it's bumpy. (And farthest away from the bus driver, of course.)

Emma has the opposite opinion about where to sit on the bus. Emma always sits in the front seat for everything—buses, classes, and even the front seat of the car. She always wants to be up front and first for everything.

I'm the twin who likes to chill in the back. Unless there's a stage involved. Then I want to be front and center. Yes, I love acting. I love being in Drama Club at school and in school plays. And when my parents let me do two clubs, I could be on camera for VOGS club. VOGS is the school's video news show.

My parents made me stop doing VOGS, though, because I bombed a test and a quiz in English. Sigh. My parents told me I had to choose between Drama Club and VOGS until I could get my grades back up. I chose drama, but I also want to be in VOGS. I loved being on the school news show and had turned out to be kind of good at being on TV. My English teacher, Mrs. Burkle, was also my drama teacher, so I was hoping to extra-impress her at Drama Club today. It couldn't hurt!

I pictured it now.

"Payton, your acting is so fabulous that I will also

give you extra credit in English class!" Mrs. Burkle would say. "A++!"

Okay, unlikely, I know. But at least I still got to be in Drama Club.

Emma wasn't in the Drama Club or VOGS club. But somehow she kept getting sucked into performing onstage and on-screen—usually pretending to be me. It had happened our very first week of school. It had happened in our school play. And it had happened on our trip to New York City.

This last twin switch was pretty epic, not only because we were on an almost-Broadway stage. We also got to get back at this girl Ashlynn who was trying to humiliate us and our classmates on our school trip.

I had been surprised to see Ashlynn. She lived in NYC, so I hadn't seen her since she tortured me at summer camp last year. Ashlynn had pretty much turned me into her slave, making me clean things in exchange for her hand-me-down clothes. At the time I'd thought it was worth it so I could look cool in middle school. Let's just say it didn't work out as planned.

But we prevailed in New York City, and now Ashlynn would never bother me again—*muah-ha-ha!*

"Why are you making those weird cackling sounds?"

A girl who had just boarded the bus stopped in the aisle and looked at me. Oh. It was Sydney. She wasn't as bad as Ashlynn, but let's just say she's not my biggest fan.

During the first week of middle school I'd thought Sydney would be the cool kind of friend to have. She was already the center of attention, had great clothes, and seemed to know all the cutest guys. Instead, she'd turned out to be a major mean girl. Especially to me. She turned on me after an incident where I'd tripped at lunch and my burrito went flying and oozed all over people.

Anyway, Sydney usually didn't ride my bus. I hoped she hadn't moved to my neighborhood and would be riding my bus permanently.

"Move," she commanded two kids who were sitting in a back seat across the aisle from me. Because she was Sydney, they obeyed and scrambled out to sit somewhere else. Sydney slid into the seat and stretched her legs out, putting her feet (in cute olive espadrilles) across the seat so nobody would sit there.

"Well, hi, Payton," Sydney said. Hmm. Sydney and I had become temporary allies versus Ashlynn in New York City. So maybe things had changed for the better.

I cautiously said hi back.

"Those kids thought they were cool enough for the

back seats. *Pfft*, I don't think so," Sydney scoffed. "But apparently, Payton, you think you are. And you think you're so cool that you even wear sunglasses on the bus."

Things had *not* changed for the better. I reached up to take my sunglasses off but realized that she'd know I cared what she said. And I didn't. *La la la, ignore.* I kept my sunglasses on. I did, however, tell myself not to make that cackling sound again. I dropped my hands and pretended to be busy looking for something important in my bag. Yes, very important.

"Are you wearing sunglasses because you think you're a major star now?" Sydney kept going. "A glamorous off-Broadway star?"

La la la, not bothering me at all.

"Or," Sydney kept going, "are you wearing sunglasses so people won't recognize you? After you and your twin totally embarrassed yourselves on school TV when you got in that huge fight, I don't blame you for trying to hide."

Oh, ugh. That was weeks ago! I was hoping everyone had forgotten about that disaster. Emma and I had started our middle school careers as the twins who had switched places, fooled everyone until they were busted, and been filmed on school television making complete idiots of themselves.

But that was supposed to be totally in the past. And I wanted to keep it that way. So I changed the subject. And if there was one topic of conversation that could distract Sydney, it was . . . Sydney.

"Sydney, why are you on my bus?" I asked her.

Sydney's face lit up.

"I slept over at my aunt and uncle's house," she said. "For a seriously exciting reason. A seriously exciting *secret* reason."

I didn't say anything.

"But if you want to know"—Sydney leaned over—"I'll give you a clue."

"That's okay," I said. "I don't need to know."

I shrugged and went back to fake-searching my tote bag. I'd gotten much better at learning how to handle Sydney. If there was something Sydney hated, it was being ignored. I leaned back in my seat so she would know that I really didn't want to know about her excitingly secret secrets. (Although I was curious.) (But *so* not worth it.)

"Payton?" Sydney gave me her squinty look. "Payton?"

Ignoring you, Sydney. Doo dee doo.

"Payton? Why is your twin sister waving her arms around freakishly?" Sydney was no longer looking at me but toward the front of the bus.

Sydney knew just how to get me to un-ignore her.

I leaned forward and looked up the aisle. Sure enough, I could see the top of my sister's head, and her hands waving wildly around above the seat. Oh no, what was she doing? I thought about ignoring her but I noticed people were also leaning forward to look at her. I pulled out my cell phone and texted.

E! Chill. Hands down.

No response. I could still see Emma's hands waving around in the air for some unknown reason. Sigh. She didn't realize it, I was sure, but she was embarrassing herself. And not just herself—us. Here was one of the major problems with being an identical twin: People didn't always know who was who. That meant people could be thinking that it was me in the front seat. Me, Payton, waving my hands wildly around and making a scene.

She must be stopped.

I fastened up my tote bag and left it on the seat so nobody would try to snag *my* back seat. I couldn't let Sydney rule my bus entirely. I did my best to ignore her as I slid out and walked up the aisle.

There went Emma's hands, waving. I could hear people cracking up as I walked up the aisle. I picked up my pace to stop her as soon as possible. However, I'd forgotten I was still wearing sunglasses, which meant I couldn't see very well. For example, I didn't see somebody's violin case sticking slightly out into the aisle until I tripped over it. I stumbled forward just as the bus lurched into a left turn.

Ack! I grabbed on to the closest seat back and accidentally yanked somebody's ponytail.

"Ouch!" The ponytail owner yelped. Loudly. Unfortunately, that meant pretty much everybody on the bus looked away from Emma's hands and saw me trip and stumble my way up the aisle, out of control. And anybody who hadn't looked yet definitely did when the bus driver yelled at me.

"You! In the sunglasses! Sit down while the bus is moving!"

I felt my face turn bright red. I quickly sat down on the edge of an empty seat and waited until the bus became more stable. Then I ducked down and half-crawled up the aisle toward my sister, trying to stay under the bus driver's radar.

I slid into the seat next to Emma, which was open because the only other person I knew who liked to sit in the front seat for everything was Jazmine James. And her mother drove her to school every day.

"Why hello, Payton," Emma said calmly, her hands now in her lap like a normal person's. "What are you doing up here in the front of the bus?"

"I'm here to ask you to stop waving your hands wildly," I whispered. "The whole bus can see you and it's embarrassing."

"More or less embarrassing than stumbling up the aisle, yanking somebody's hair, and getting yelled at by Morris, the bus driver?" Emma peered at me. "While wearing oversize sunglasses on a bleak day?"

Agh! I slumped back on the seat in defeat.

"I was hoping you didn't notice my approach," I said.

"Of course I saw it. I see everything on this bus," Emma said. She pointed to a large mirror that was attached to the back of the bus driver's seat. "I convinced Morris to angle an additional mirror so that I can monitor the goings-on of my fellow bus mates. This way I can alert him to any shenanigans."

"Are you serious?" I asked her.

"Oh, she's very serious," the bus driver chimed in.

"Oh, Morris, does this mean I can speak now?" Emma called up to the driver.

"No," Morris replied.

Emma saluted him and made a "zip up her lips" motion.

What the heck?

"I'm no longer allowed to speak to Morris when the bus is moving," Emma explained. "I had been trying to help him out by telling him about shortcuts he could take. I also alerted him when he was waiting too long for a student, which might put him behind schedule. And I told him when people behind us were causing distractions."

"She was very distracting," Morris grumbled.

Emma sighed. "So we made a deal that I could stay in the front seat if I didn't talk to him without him calling on me first. I came up with the idea to wave to him to alert him when I have valuable information to share."

The bus turned into a neighborhood as Emma continued speaking.

"So I'm honing my nonverbal skills in the process. Did you know that spoken language is less than one-third of our communication? Most of our feelings and intentions are sent through body language." Emma waved her arms wildly, I guess to demonstrate. "Or hand gestures." She gave me a thumbs-up. "And facial expressions. For example, I'm copying your facial expression right now, Payton. It's a cross between a scowl and a look of frustration. Thus, I'm inferring that you are irritated by something."

"Or someone." I sighed. Morris the bus driver sighed too.

Morris probably ignored Emma half the time, like Dad did when Emma sat in the front seat and tried to tell him more effective driving methods. Emma likes to point out when things could be done better. Yes, it could be annoying. But I had to admit, she was almost always right.

The bus slowed down and pulled up to a bus stop. A bunch of kids got on the bus.

"Okay, I get it," I told Emma. "But can you not wave your hands so very wildly? It looks pretty spazzy and we can even see you all the way in the back. People might think you're me."

I hoped she would get the hint that she was embarrassing us.

"And, Payton," Emma said, "would you mind following the bus safety rules by not walking while the bus is in motion? People might think *you* are *me* breaking a rule. That would be so embarrassing."

I groaned. I couldn't win.

"And speaking of spazzy," Emma continued, "people are still talking about you stumbling down the aisle."

"How do you know that?" I asked her.

"I can see them in the rearview mirror." Emma pointed. "As you know, I've been practicing reading lips. That girl with the slate-gray stylishly tied scarf just said something about how you're wearing sunglasses on the bus like you're a TV star. And then she laughed, remembering how we got into that fight the first week on school TV."

I groaned again. This was not going as planned.

"I'm going back to my seat," I said.

"If you need to tell me anything else," Emma said, "just wave your hands wildly from your seat and get my attention. Then mouth it. I need more practice reading lips."

"Can't you just use twin telepathy?" I tried one last-ditch effort. "Practice reading my mind instead?"

"Payton, shh. You're not supposed to be talking to me out loud, remember?" Emma replied. Then she mouthed something at me that I completely didn't understand.

I felt defeated as I slid my sunglasses off and waited for the bus to stop so I could go back to my seat. The bus slowed down and pulled to a stop and the doors whooshed open. I stood up and started walking to the back. But not before I saw Emma's hand go up and wave.

"Yes, Emma?" I heard Morris say.

"You don't have to wait for him," Emma replied. "He's a minute late and you're already two minutes behind schedule."

I looked out the window to see a boy in my Drama Club, Sam, running madly to catch the bus. I turned back to Emma.

"Sam is carrying a prop for our Drama Club skit," I said to Emma. "It's slowing him down. Give him a break."

Sam was carrying a beach chair that was big and awkward. I was glad I had only brought sunglasses. I waited at the front to make sure Emma couldn't convince the driver to leave him.

"Made it!" Sam said, huffing and puffing as he climbed up the steps.

"An extra one minute and twelve seconds delay," Emma said, shaking her head.

I sighed as I stood up and followed Sam down the aisle. It was slow going, as he banged into people with the beach chair as he passed by.

"Can I go ahead of you?" I asked him. "I already got yelled at by the driver once for being in the aisle."

"Sure!" Sam said cheerfully, and as he stood to the side he knocked another person on the side of the head.

"Sorry," I told them. "Sorry!"

I was relieved to slide into my back seat without stumbling or pulling anyone's hair myself.

"Are you okay?" Sydney asked. "I saw you falling all over the place."

Ugh. I had forgotten all about Sydney being on my bus. I slid my sunglasses back on so I could ignore her.

"Did you bruise anything?" she continued in a voice of mock concern. "Or just your ego?"

A few seconds later I had a brief moment of happy karma when Sam made his way to the back and tried to sit with Sydney. When she told him the seat was saved, he got up and the beach chair accidentally knocked her on the side of the head.

"Can I sit with you?" Sam asked me.

"Sure," I said, and moved my tote bag. Sam tried to wedge himself and the beach chair into the seat. It was a tight fit.

"Sorry to squish you," Sam apologized.

"It's okay," I said. "Well, if you could get the top of the chair out of my stomach it will be okay."

"Sorry." Sam shifted the chair. "This bus is lame. It

would be cool if we could have a huge double-decker bus like we went on in New York City."

"I know! That bus was cool," I said. Emma and I had sat on the top out in the open air.

Brzzzzt. Bzzzt.

Speaking of Emma, my cell went off. Emma was texting me.

Look up and say something. I angled the mirror 76 degrees so I can read your lips perfectly.

I shook my head, my lips tightly closed.

Brzzzzt. Bzzzt.

Shaking head doesn't count! Say something! I want to prove to u my mad lip-reading skillz.

I mouthed: *You are bizarre.*

Brzzzzt. Bzzzt.

You said "You are star!" ☺ Twin-kle twin-kle little star 2 u!

Sigh. I started to slide my phone back into my bag.

Brzzzzt. Bzzzt.

What now? I pulled up her text and read it.

But you may want to take off your sunglasses. They're kind of embarrassing.

Ag. I gave up.

Emma

Two

ON THE WAY TO SIXTH-PERIOD STUDY HALL

My lip balm! Did I remember to bring my lip balm?

I slipped my hand into the outside pockets of my backpack. I felt my mechanical pencils (eraser side up), sticky notes (sticky side up, ew), and my extra scrunchie. A cinnamon-raisin granola bar for after school.

And, whew, my lip balm. I pulled out the vanilla-flavored stick from pocket #4. Normally, I didn't wear any cosmetics. Unless Payton forced me to wear lip gloss on "special occasions." Which, for her, was every day at school. Or at home. My twin sister was a lip gloss expert.

I, however, was a lip-*reading* expert. Well, not exactly an expert—but I was picking it up pretty quickly. Like on the bus earlier this morning, I could tell that people were talking about my twin's massive wipeout on the bus. Not by listening, but by reading their lips!

Although you couldn't miss their laughter.

Anyway, Payton may be a little spazzy, but she's my best friend. A few weeks ago I might have said she's my *only* friend in my peer group. But then middle school happened. Now I had friends. And I was back in my familiar environs. Yup. It was going to be a normal day.

"What's the capital of Loserland?" a familiar and unwelcome voice said behind me. "Millsville!"

I turned around.

Jazmine James!

"Get it? 'Cause your last name is Mills?" A boy's voice.

And her sidekick, Hector!

"And that's where Emma will be after the geography bee." Jazmine cackled. "Millsville, Loserland!"

Sigh. I turned around from my locker. Besides making friends in middle school, I'd also made a few enemies. I leaned back casually. *Don't let her get to you.*

"Still hurting after I annihilated you at the mathletes competition?" I faced Jazmine and Hector. "The competition that I *won?*"

"Oh, please." Jazmine waved dismissively. "That was so last weekend."

Last weekend we were in New York City! Now we were back to the usual routine. Which I liked. "Predictable" was my favorite word. Besides "winner."

Riinnnng! The warning bell rang.

"Well, lovely talking to you, but I must go," I said, shutting my locker door and turning to head to study hall . . . *YANK!*

"OW!" I shrieked as I was slammed backward into my locker. My ponytail. I'd closed my locker on my hair. I tugged. Nothing happened. I was stuck. I was stuck in my locker.

"Heh," said Hector. Then he and Jazmine burst into hysterical laughter and went off down the hallway. Jazmine's long braids swung freely down her back and she treated the hall as her personal catwalk, elbowing people out of her way when they got too close.

Grrr. Jazmine James. From Eviltown.

"Hi, whichever twin you are!" a girl called to me as she walked by.

"Uh—hi!" I said. I leaned back against my locker, so maybe I'd look like I was hanging out. *La la la, keeep moving, folks. Nothing to see here.*

"Hi, Payton!" another girl said to me.

"Er—hi!" I said. Thanks to a public humiliation after our first twin switch, Payton and I had become rather well-known. Although most people couldn't tell us apart. But hey, that was good in this case. They could think my *twin* was plastered to her locker. Payton, not Emma.

"Hey, Emma!" my friend Quinn greeted me.

"Quinn!" I yelled. "Can you, um, come here for a second?"

Quinn stopped and frowned a little.

"Can we talk later?" she asked. "I don't want to be late for class."

"Please?" I begged.

Quinn came over quickly.

"I'm stuck," I admitted. "My hair is stuck in my locker."

"Ow, does it hurt?" Quinn asked, looking concerned.

Note to self: Friends don't laugh when you're in trouble. Unlike Jazmenemies.

"Only if I move," I said. "I tried to pull it out, but I got nowhere."

"Okay," Quinn said. "What's your locker combination?"

"Great idea!" I told her the numbers. And I tried to smile, in case the people walking by saw me in this stupid situation. The very last thing I wanted was for people to think "stupid" and "Emma Mills" at the same time.

"Forty-nine . . . sixteen . . . three," Quinn repeated. I heard the wheel spinning. "How do you remember your combination? I'm terrible remembering numbers."

"The square root of forty-nine is seven, minus the square root of sixteen, which is four, equals three," I said. "Did it work?"

"Oh, sorry, I forgot to turn it twice," she answered. "What was it again?"

I told her. Perhaps even merely a month ago, I would have rolled my eyes. But having a nice friend like Quinn had upped my social skills from "zero" to . . . well, improving.

"Got it!" Quinn said triumphantly, and I heard a *click*.

"I'm free!" I said, shaking out my ponytail. Crisis over.

"Yay," said Quinn. "Now I've gotta go. Can you hang out after school?"

"No." I sighed. "I'm tutoring today." I thought about my new outlook on friends. I wanted them. So I made sure Quinn knew I wasn't just blowing her off.

"Quinn, I want to hang out, so let's plan something more fun than rescuing me from a—er—hairy situation. Like a Boggle tournament or the mall."

Quinn smiled and nodded as she left.

Well, I handled that well. Considering I'd been stuck in a locker, that is. Which, yikes, made me late for study hall! I rushed to study hall. Fortunately, it was in the same hallway as my locker. And since I had to tutor Mason and Jason, the Trouble Twins, after school, I needed every spare moment to study in study hall. I was on an intense study mission for my next competition: the Geobee! The schoolwide competition was Friday night and I was going to be ready for it. *Geobee, Geobee, geography is fun for me . . . especially when I win.*

And with that happy thought, I walked into study hall just in time before the last bell rang. I had exactly forty-three minutes to prepare for the competition. I planned to answer every question correctly. Emma = 100 percent winner!

Payton

Three

"The next student to answer this question correctly will receive a Burkle bonus point," Mrs. Burkle announced to the class.

I was in my English/language arts class. Mrs. Burkle was both Emma's and my E/LA teacher as well as Drama Club advisor. And yay, there were only three more periods to go until Drama Club.

I perked up at the thought of a Burkle bonus point. That meant you got a get-out-of-homework-although-not-a-test-free card you could use anytime that year. I could use one of those, especially when we got busy with a new play!

"A rare opportunity, this," Mrs. Burkle called out. "A Burkle bonus point and a chance to impress The Burkle!"

I really needed to impress Burkle. I'd made an impression on her, but it was partly because of our twin switch fiascos. Sure, she'd been happy with me in New York City, but when I got back I messed up a quiz and a test. Ouch. School had gotten even harder for me now, and not just because I was in middle school. This year, for the first time, Emma wasn't in any of my classes. Before, if the teacher called on me and I didn't know the answer, she was always there to wave her hand around and rescue me.

Also, Emma could sense when I was spacing out and would poke me with one of her freshly sharpened pencils. Yes, this year was much less painful but also more pressured.

I really wanted to get my grades up and get back into VOGS. I really liked being on camera. And I liked the cameraman, too . . . Nick! He ran the crew for both Drama Club and VOGS. Hee hee!

"Okay, class. The question is . . ."

I shot my hand up even before she asked the question so she couldn't miss me.

"What was the theme of the story?"

Crumbcakes. Theme was tricky and I was never exactly sure. I dropped my hand, defeated. I listened as another girl answered the question and got the Burkle bonus point.

It was times like these that I wished I had Emma's brain. Most of the time I was okay with being the normal kind of school smart. But every now and then I was jealous that Emma could answer hard questions like stuff about story themes and college-level calculus. Whatever that is. It's not like I wanted to be in the advanced classes and have to compete against the Jazmine Jameses of the world but . . . a Burkle bonus point once in a while might be nice.

Sigh.

"Let's discuss the conflict of the story," Mrs. Burkle said. "Conflict can be man against man, man against nature—" Then a buzzing noise came from her desk.

Bzzzt. Bzzzt.

"Man against himself," she said. *Bzzzt.*

"Man against cell phone," someone called out, and everyone laughed.

"They aren't giving up, are they?" Mrs. Burkle sighed. "Pardon me." She pulled out a cell phone from her desk and looked at it. Then I swear she looked right at me. She nodded and texted and then put her phone on her desk.

"Uh, now where was I?" Burkle went back into teacher mode. "Ah, yes. Conflict. In chapter five . . ."

Her cell phone buzzed again. She stopped talking and picked it up. This time her eyes widened as she read her phone. Then I swear she looked up and looked right at me *again*.

No, I was probably just being paranoid. Teachers didn't usually text in class. But I guess there was no rule against it like there was for the students, who would have their cell phones confiscated and kept in the principal's office till the end of the day.

Burkle put her cell phone in her blazer pocket and started talking to the class again. But yet again her cell phone buzzed and this time she actually let out a giggle when she read it. And then she looked in my direction again.

The girl behind me tapped me on the shoulder. "What's Burkle doing?"

"Texting?" I whispered back, shrugging.

"I mean, why does Burkle keep looking at you?"

So I wasn't being paranoid. I shifted uncomfortably

in my seat. That was the last time Mrs. Burkle used her phone, but I swear when I was filling out my short-answer form she gave me a couple of squinty looks.

I pretended not to notice and to be a perfect student so she would stop giving me weird looks and instead start thinking, *Look at Payton, a hardworking student who deserves to be in both the Drama Club and VOGS, oh yes.*

"Payton," Mrs. Burkle's voice rang out through the classroom. "I request your presence at my desk."

Everyone was looking at me like, *Ooh, somebody's in trouble.* SO much trouble that the teacher gave them weird looks all through class. Oh no. This was the exact opposite of what I needed.

I slunk up to her desk and blurted out, "I'm sorry, Mrs. Burkle." I babbled on. "I didn't mean it. It was a mistake. I'll never do it again."

Mrs. Burkle peered at me somewhat strangely. She slid her rectangular glasses off of her nose and leaned in toward me.

"Payton," she said. "What did you do?"

"Um." I fidgeted. "I have no idea. But it must have been bad because you were looking at me funny all class."

Mrs. Burkle let out a laugh.

"Oh heavens, I hadn't realized you'd noticed," Burkle

said. "I thought I was being stealthy. Well, let's move along now and get on with it. Class, my teacher's aide, Mr. LaPerna, is on his way here to supervise while I am gone. Please be on good behavior, as his blood sugar issues can cause him to be cranky at this time of day."

Burkle got up and started walking out the door.

"Excuse me," I said, and followed her. "Mrs. Burkle? Where are we going?"

"To Counselor Case's office!" she said. "Come, come. No dillydallying. This is almost my lunch period, and rumor has it somebody brought oatmeal cookies to the teachers' lounge."

I didn't say anything, but here's what I was thinking: *Counselor Case's office?* I had only gone to my guidance counselor's office when I was busted for twin switches. Oh no, did she find out that Emma and I had traded places in New York City? Were we going to be in belated trouble? I wondered what my punishment would be. Maybe I'd have to be a drama servant, cleaning under the stage again. Oh no!

I followed Mrs. Burkle into Counselor Case's office and the assistant told us it would be just a minute.

"Where is that sister of yours?" Burkle asked, looking around. "I wonder if she got the message."

"Emma is coming?" I shifted in my seat nervously. That confirmed my worst fear. We were both in trouble. Twin-Switch Trouble. I slumped in my chair. Why oh why did we switch? Most of our switching had been by accident! Or because we were desperate! Oh, good-bye Drama Club, good-bye my hopes to be in VOGS. Hello under the stage for me, and probably more Mason and Jason for Emma.

"Where is that twin of yours? I better go track her down," Burkle said. "You stay here."

As soon as she was gone, I reached into my tote bag and felt for my phone. I had to warn Emma!

Emma

Four

SIXTH-PERIOD STUDY HALL

Psst.

What was that hissing sound? I ignored it and took my Geobee handbook and notecards out of my back-pack.

Cough cough "Emma" *cough*.

I looked up and to the right. It was Sam the Munch-kin. He mouthed something to me. The study hall monitor was strict—no talking. But this was timely—an opportunity to read lips.

Hair, he was saying.

Oh no. Did Sam see me get my hair stuck?

Hair! Oh no. Was my hair messed up? My hand flew

to my ponytail. I felt the strands. No tangles. Nothing sticking out. *Whew.*

I wasn't vain about my looks or anything, but I *was* the twin with the extra-shiny hair. (Payton was the twin with the bigger nose.)

"Em!" Sam whispered. He was wiggling his eyebrows and pointing at my foot. What? The only non-verbal communication I was learning was lip-reading.

"HERE!" he said.

Oh. *Here!* Not hair.

I looked down at my foot. On top of my comfy (but cute) sneaker was a square of paper. I knew, of course, that note-passing was common amongst my peers, but it was a ritual I had little experience with.

I carefully leaned over and picked up the folded square. I opened it. *Just saying hey! See you, Ox.* I would suspend my disclaim of social note-passing just this once. Because Ox was . . .

Brzzzzt!

What??? My phone? Someone was texting me—during school! That was totally not allowed! I was going to get in so much trouble!

First I was passed a note, now I'm getting a text? This was study hall, not social hour, people!!! I grabbed my phone and answered it before it buzzed again.

It was a text from Payton. We had agreed only to text during school in Extreme Emergency.

Waiting for u in Case's office. We must be in trouble. Burkle coming to get u.

What???

We?

If "we" were in trouble—it could only mean one thing. It was something *we* did together.

A twin switch.

But which one?

When we were in Times Square in New York City? Or one of our others? We never *planned* to switch. Or meant to cause trouble. Oh, this was not good.

"Em—*crackle*—Mills, please report—*crinklecrackle*—guidance office," a voice boomed out from the classroom intercom.

Everyone turned to look at me. I felt my face turn red.

I quickly scooped up my stuff and went up to the study hall monitor to get a hall pass. And then I was out the door, on my way to find out what was going on.

Exactly two minutes later, I entered Counselor Case's office. My twin was sitting in one of the chairs.

"What's going on?" I asked Payton, and plunked

down on a chair next to her. Payton just looked at me and frowned. She reached into her tote bag and pulled out . . . a hairbrush.

"We've been called into the counselor's office, and we may be in major trouble, and you're worried about your *hair*?" I said in disbelief.

"Not *my* hair," Payton said. "*Yours.* You look like you've just run a marathon. Your hair is sprouting out of your ponytail and sticking up in, like, five different places."

"*Sigh.*" I sighed, letting her know how mixed up her priorities were. But still. I took the brush and redid my ponytail, smoothing out the flyaways.

"So, is this about a switch?" Payton asked.

"I don't know," I told her. "But I'm afraid it probably is. I just passed Counselor Case outside in the hallway. She was talking to Mrs. Burkle, and it was *very* tempting." I gave Payton back the brush, my hand trembling a bit. Oh no. Was I going to have an anxiety attack?

"What was tempting?" Payton asked.

"I started to read their lips," I admitted. "Then I realized how wrong that would be. Did you know the ethics of lip-reading are rather amorphous?" *Breathe out slowly.*

"Emma!" my sister said. "In English! What are you talking about?"

"I saw Counselor Case say the words 'identical twins,'" I said. "And then the words 'smelly wood.'" *Breathe in.* I began the calming technique I used in sudden-death final rounds of competitions. Which I usually won. *Breathe out.*

"Smelly wood?" Payton wrinkled her nose.

"Yup. Smelly wood," I said. "And then Counselor Case replied 'jolly good.' Payton, I think I'm going to have a panic attack! I can't be in trouble now! I've got the geography bee coming up this weekend!"

"Emma," my twin said, "breathe in and breathe out slowly. You've got to remain calm."

We were quiet for a moment while I inhaled and exhaled.

"Oh no!" Payton shrieked suddenly. "Smelly wood must have something to do with our punishment! It probably means I have to do something smelly—like under the stage for Drama Club. Or maybe I have to build heavy things for the sets out of smelly wood! And Counselor Case thinks that would be a jolly good punishment. Oh, this is awful! I just got *out* from under the stage!"

"That's pretty weak," I told her.

"Then maybe it is about *your* punishment," she said. "Maybe Burkle meant something smelly would be *your* punishment—like extra tutoring time with stinky boys!"

"Mason and Jason do like to fart a lot," I agreed. "But why would Counselor Case say 'jolly good' after Mrs. Burkle just called her sons smelly?"

Mason and Jason were Counselor Case's eight-year-old twins. I tutor them for community service, as punishment for our first twin switch.

"I don't knooooow!" Payton wailed. "I'm so upset!"

"I'm hyperventilating!" I moaned.

Neither of us had noticed that Counselor Case and Mrs. Burkle had entered the room.

That's just what I like to see," Mrs. Burkle announced, looking at us.

Payton and I stopped our noise and looked at each other. This was worse than I thought. They wanted to see us miserable?

"You like to see us wailing? And moaning?" I blurted out.

"Dramatic twins!" Mrs. Burkle said. "I like to see dramatic twins."

"It does help confirm what we were talking about."

Counselor Case nodded. "I do believe your friend made the right decision, Bertha."

What were they talking about? I couldn't stand the suspense anymore. I needed to know the punishment, the consequences, and the penalties.

"With all due respect," I spoke up. "I believe my head will explode if you don't tell me what is going to happen to us."

And then something unexpected happened. Mrs. Burkle and Counselor Case looked at each other and smiled. Then they looked at us and smiled.

"Do you remember how I told you I met my dear friend Jane in performing arts school?" Mrs. Burkle asked us.

"Jane, the director of the off-Broadway show from our trip to New York City?" Payton asked her.

"Correct," Mrs. Burkle said, and then she clasped her hands over her heart. "Jane and I had another friend in college, a chap named Lewis. We were the best of friends. Jane, Bertha, and Lewis. We were the Three Musketeers, the terrific trio, the inseparable three, the—"

"Ahem." Counselor Case cleared her throat. "I believe we get the picture, Bertha."

"Yes, well," Burkle said. "Jane, as you know, moved

 36

to New York City. I moved here to mold and shape young minds in a scholarly environment. Lewis went west to seek fame and fortune. Lewis is a casting director in Los Angeles. Jane, Lewis, and I were having our monthly group chat on Skype and Jane and I told her about our delightful adventures in Manhattan. And something piqued Lewis's interest."

I was clueless. And that didn't happen often in my life.

"We were telling Lewis about your performance and improvisation. It turns out he is casting a commercial that features identical twins. I e-mailed a video clip of you girls that Jane had taken."

"With your parents' permission," Counselor Case interjected. "Signed."

"Lewis and the client loved you two. They want you to star in their commercial."

My jaw dropped. Payton's jaw dropped. And we both said at the exact same time:

"He wants us to what?!"

Mrs. Burkle and Counselor Case both laughed.

"That was such a perfect identical twin moment," Burkle said. "This was a quality Lewis could see in you two."

"So we're seriously going to be in a commercial?" Payton gasped. "Like a commercial on TV and on the Internet that people can actually watch?"

"Or fast forward through," I pointed out, but everyone ignored me.

"Absolutely, Payton," Counselor Case said. "This is such an exciting opportunity, not only to perform but to continue expanding your horizons with travel."

"Travel?" Payton and I both spoke in unison again, which made Mrs. Burkle and Counselor Case laugh again.

"Yes, didn't I mention Lewis works in Los Angeles, California?"

Yes, but . . . wait a minute. She couldn't mean . . .

"Emma and Payton, you are going to Hollywood," our drama teacher said dramatically.

"Hollywood? No. No way!" Payton squealed.

"Yes. Yes way," Mrs. Burkle said, clapping her hands together.

Hollywood?

"Squee!" Payton squealed and jumped up from the chair. "Squee! Eeee! Yay!"

She grabbed my hands and tried to do a happy dance. But I just sat there.

"Emma, we're going to Hollywood to be in a commercial! A commercial starring identical twins! Like us!"

Well, that part was perfect casting. Payton and I look as identical as two twins could. Other than my hair, which was shinier, of course.

But the Mills Twins going to . . . Hollywood?!

Hmm.

"Emma! Why don't you look excited? This is huge! This is unbelievable!" Payton said. Counselor Case and Mrs. Burkle both looked at me quizzically as well.

"I agree this is unbelievable," I replied calmly. "And with all due respect, highly suspicious. You mean to tell me that with all of the thousands of actors already auditioning in Hollywood, they would need to fly us out there?"

Payton had stopped jumping around and was just looking at me.

"What?" I looked calmly at the three of them. "We're two girls with no professional experience, talent agent, manager, or mom-ager. Why us? Suspicious, isn't it?"

"It's Mrs. Burkle's BFF!" Payton cried out.

I turned to Mrs. Burkle. "He couldn't find identical twins in Hollywood?" Mrs. Burkle smiled.

"I understand your concerns," she said. "And I agree

that this is highly unusual. However, I have an explanation. Lewis did audition many sets of twins, but he told me he was looking for, in his words, 'real girls.' Not trained actresses or supermodels, but real girls."

"See, Emma?" Payton said.

"So I told him about the two of you. He enjoyed my story about your little switching-places escapades. He thought you girls would be a refreshing addition to the shampoo commercial."

A shampoo commercial? Well now things were starting to make a little more sense to me. Our best feature was our shiny hair.

"Well," I admitted, "I do have unnaturally natural shiny hair. Payton, remember the time Mason's pet gecko jumped on my head because he was so attracted to my hair under the fluorescent lighting?"

"Yeah, whatever." Payton waved that away. Poor thing was still in denial that her hair wasn't the shiniest. "But you're missing the point here."

"A shampoo commercial." I needed to consider this carefully. "In Hollywood. Well, I must confess I'm tempted, but I'll need a little time to weigh the pros and cons."

"Unfortunately one thing you do not have is time,"

Mrs. Burkle said. "The commercial shoot is in two days. Your father is on his way to pick you both up. You fly out tomorrow morning."

"Tomorrow morning?" Payton and I said at the same time. Except Payton was smiling and I was frowning.

"I'm sorry." I shrugged. "I'll be unavailable. I can't go."

"WHAT?!" Payton, Mrs. Burkle, and Counselor Case gasped in unison. For a moment, it was like they were identical triplets with their mouths hanging open as they gaped at me. I was sorry to disappoint, but this was just too last-minute.

"Well," I explained. "Would we be home by Saturday?"

"I hope not!" Payton said. "Emma, it's Hollywood! Who wouldn't want to stay as long as possible?"

"Me," I said, sitting back and folding my arms.

"I believe you'd be there two nights at least," Mrs. Burkle said. "If you're worried about expenses, the whole trip will be paid for."

"That's not it," I said.

"That's amazing," my twin sister said at the same time.

I looked at Payton. Payton looked at me. Absolutely no twin ESP was happening.

"The schoolwide Geobee is Saturday!" I said. How could anyone forget? Sure, winning the mathletes competition last week was amazing. But that was last week, and this was this week. That was math and this was geography.

Besides, I couldn't let Jazmine James win. Anything. Ever.

"Wait a moment, Emma," Counselor Case said. "I think you're missing the big picture here."

"Counselor Case," I said. "Winning the geography bee will be a valuable addition to my resume. You, of course, would support my decision."

"I do see your point, but there will be many opportunities for Geobees. And the spelling bee is in a few weeks, and I'm guessing you'll enter the science fair."

Yes, but if Jazmine James wins, she'll wear her Geobee T-shirt to class and rub it in my face. You're only as good as your last competition. No-show equals nobody.

"Emma." My guidance counselor/part-time employer leaned forward in her chair and looked directly at me. "When you are up onstage in front of a national audience, television cameras all aimed at you, as you prepare to win a competition—how much more prepared will you be if you've already been in a commercial? Imagine the advantage you'll have."

I was imagining. Everybody saying, "Emma Mills is brilliant, poised, *and* she's famous for her shiny hair." That would impress—and intimidate—everybody, including Jazmine Janes *and* college admissions counselors. . . .

"Okay," I said. "I'll do it."

"Eeeeeeee!" Payton shrieked. "We're going to Hollywood!"

"Yes, you are," Mrs. Burkle said, clasping her hands together. "Tomorrow morning! Your father will be here shortly to fill out some paperwork, and then you are both excused from school on work release."

"Work?" Payton said. "Does that mean we get paid?"

"Release?" I said. "Does that mean I have to leave early?"

"Er, we'll wait for your father to discuss all the details, Payton," Mrs. Burkle said. "And yes, Emma, you're allowed to leave early."

"No, thank you," I said politely. "I'd rather stay at school and go home on the bus." I had advanced math last period and, of course I didn't want to miss that.

"That is so dedicated of you." Counselor Case smiled. "To not miss tutoring my Mason and Jason!"

Um, yeah, I thought. *That, too.*

"And I want to stay also," Payton said. "I'm in a skit in Drama Club. I've got my prop ready." She pulled a pair of sunglasses out of her tote bag and showed Mrs. Burkle.

"Very dedicated." Mrs. Burkle beamed. "And fabulous for Hollywood."

"Ooh!" Payton put them on and did a movie-star pose.

Then Counselor Case signed our hall passes. "Congratulations, girls," she said, and sent us out.

As soon as we were out the door, Payton squeed.

"I! Can't! Believe! It!" my twin sister said, somehow managing to speak in exclamation points. Genetically, I suppose that meant I could too, but I didn't have any urge to try.

"Me neither," I said, shaking my head. "How did I forget about tutoring the Terror Twins? Well, at least the money will come in handy."

"You know what I meant," Payton said. "By the way, what do *you* need? New batteries for your calculator?"

"No, new sunglasses," I replied, starting to enjoy the idea of Hollywood. "I'm thinking: large, round, mysterious-but-intelligent. Mathlete meets movie star!" I struck a pose. Or something.

We both started cracking up. Then we both looked at each other.

"We're going to Hollywood!" Payton said. We hugged and headed in different directions to get to our next classes.

"Emma!" Payton called out. I turned back to catch her mouthing something.

Jolly good? Smelly wood?

Oh! *Now* I understood: HOLLYWOOD!

Five

SCHOOL HALLWAY

I'm going to Hollywood! Where celebrities live and work! Where movies, television shows, and shampoo commercials are filmed! I did my little happy dance, right there in the hallway in front of my locker.

"Nice moves, Twin." Sydney and Cashmere walked up to me, swishing the pom-poms they always carried. "You should try out for cheer squad."

Cashmere giggled.

I can't! I thought. *I'm too busy GOING TO HOLLY-WOOD.* But I didn't say that out loud.

"Cashmere and I are out of class today because we're running the table for homecoming tickets next period,"

Sydney explained, even though I hadn't asked. "I'm going to be the homecoming representative for our grade."

She looked at me smugly, obviously hoping for a negative reaction. But no! Even homecoming made me smile, because I'm going with Nick! Yay! But looking happy in front of Sydney was a mistake. She couldn't leave without trying to bring me down.

"So now I'm a cheerleader, homecoming representative, and . . ." Sydney was talking in her syrupy-sweet voice. "I never did get to tell you my big news! I, Sydney Fish, am the new face of Tire Heaven! I'm going to film the commercial this weekend and it will be shown on two to three local cable channels!"

"Isn't that epic?" Cashmere gushed. "Sydney is going to be famous! Maybe the commercial will run on the Internet and she'll get discovered off YouTube like Dustin Weaver did!"

Cashmere held up her Dustin Weaver notebook covered in I ♥ DUSTIN stickers and squealed.

Commercials and celebrities and *squee!* Hollywood! I was in such a happy Hollywood bubble, even Sydney couldn't burst my mood.

"That's really exciting, Sydney," I told her. "Drama Geckos on television! Awesome!"

Sydney opened her mouth to say something, then frowned. She whipped around and tottered away on her high-heeled wedges, Cashmere following right behind her.

"What just happened?" I heard Cashmere ask. "I'm confused. How come she kept being nice?"

"Just keep walking," Sydney said.

Hee. I just confused Sydney with my niceness. *Kill them with kindness,* hee. It was always fun to mess with the mean girls. I got my math books and prepared to go to class. Ugh. Math. However, I had already missed half the class because of my meeting.

Messing with Sydney's head! Going to Hollywood! Missing half of math class!

I danced down the hallway to class.

Emma

Six

SCHOOL HALLWAY

The more I thought about it, the more excited I got. Travel is educational. This was a wonderful opportunity to broaden my horizons. Payton was right. Going to Hollywood was a squee.

I practically danced down the hallway toward my next class. Then the only thing better than being in class happened—I ran into Ox!

OX! The good-looking, popular athlete/mathlete who is still—shockingly—my unofficial sort-of boyfriend. Unofficial and sort-of due to our parents saying we're too young for dating, plus our focus on academics (both of us) and athletics (Ox). (Although I may consider dabbling in water polo this winter, due to an excellent overhand serve and the extracurricular credits that would look good on my college applications.)

"What are you doing here?" I asked, flustered.

"I had to leave class early to work at a table to sell homecoming dance tickets," Ox said. "Football team duty. Am I lucky and you're out of class for the same reason and going to work the table with me? Is the Geobee team required too?"

"That would be fun." I smiled. I had a nice fleeting vision of me and Ox, sitting side by side at the table, organizing the tickets and collecting money together. But no. "I just had a meeting with Counselor Case and Mrs. Burkle and got some surprising news. *Really* surprising. But it means that I won't be competing in the Geobee. I'll be out of town . . . approximately three thousand miles out of town."

"Hmm. Judging from your smile and the fact that you were practically dancing down the hallway, I'm guessing it's a good thing that's happening three thousand miles away?" Ox said.

"I was not dancing," I said. "I don't dance."

"Oh," said Ox. "Does that mean you won't dance with me at the homecoming dance?"

"Uh—" I backtracked. "I mean, I don't dance down middle-school hallways. I do dance at middle-school dances."

Ox had already asked me to the homecoming dance. And I had accepted!

"Cool," Ox said. And smiled at me.

"Cool." I smiled. "It's also cool that you could tell by my nonverbal communication that I am pleased about the surprise turn of events in my schedule."

I'd told Ox over the phone last night that I was working on nonverbal communication skills for a science project. Like how facial expressions and body language could "talk" as much as words.

"It must be something great to make you give up the Geobee," Ox said. "And dance down the hallway."

I told him my news.

"You're right. That is an amazing opportunity," Ox said after I filled him in. And then he took my hand.

Eeee!

The whole world could read *that* kind of nonverbal communication. It said, *Ox likes Emma!* Sadly, the whole world was still in class.

It felt so comfortable, so natural for me to be holding hands with him. I'd come a l-o-o-ng way since the first day of middle school, when I couldn't even speak to a boy. . . .

"Oh no!" a girl's voice cried out from behind us. "Somebody save him! He's getting away!"

What? I turned around to look for some poor guy in trouble. Instead I saw Cashmere. Admittedly not my favorite person, but she did look upset.

"Twin! Whichever twin you are!" she shrieked. "He's near your foot!"

Ox let go of my hand, leaned down, and picked up a flat, circular pin that had rolled into my foot. I caught a glimpse of a boy's face on the pin before Cashmere snatched it out of Ox's hand.

She had got to be kidding me. My hand-holding moment was ruined by a Dustin Weaver pin?

"You saved my Dustin pin! That's an exclusive pin solely for the first one thousand überfans on his website! It's precious to me!" Cashmere gushed. "Thanks, Ox! And thanks, Twin!"

She gazed at the pin in her hand.

"You're welcome," I muttered.

"Hey, do you guys know where we're supposed to have the table to sell homecoming tickets?" Cashmere asked. "I lost Sydney when my Dustin pin rolled away."

"Cafeteria," Ox told her.

"Okay, who did I just save?" Ox asked me, laughing a little as he watched Cashmere walk away, clutching her pin.

"That was Dustin Weaver, dreamy pop singer, number one on the music charts," I told him.

"Did you just call him 'dreamy'?" Ox looked at me.

"Not me personally." I rolled my eyes. "That's just what the magazines always say. 'Dustin is so dreamy!' Of course, they're not *my* magazines. They're Payton's."

I did not mention that I also read them to find out about the latest fashion and style trends. Which was an unlikely interest I'd had since Payton and I had done our first twin switch and I'd gotten stuck shopping at the mall with Cashmere and her Queen Bee BFF, Sydney. Along with my previously unknown talent for fashion, I'd gained a new friend in Quinn that day.

I had a boy friend and a girl friend. I was no longer Academma, the antisocial study-a-holic. I sighed happily.

"Thinking about your dreamy singer?" Ox teased.

"No!" I blushed. "I was thinking about . . ." I couldn't say I was thinking about *him*. Too embarrassing.

"About celebrity culture these days," I blurted. "I

mean, why do people care about celebrities? They're just people. Celebrities, I mean."

That was brilliant, Emma.

"I don't know." Ox shrugged. "I like this one model-turned-Academy-Award–winning-actress. Have you heard of Finnola Simms?"

I felt a strange emotion switch on inside me as I envisioned Ox walking with this tall, gorgeous movie star hand in hand down a red carpet.

Jealousy. Yep. That was it.

"No," I said through gritted teeth. "Who is Finnola Simms?"

"She played Abraham Lincoln's wife in my favorite History Channel show," Ox said. "She's a big animal activist in real life. I donated my Tooth Fairy money to her wildlife refuge when I was little."

"Oh, that is so cute," I said, totally relieved. Abe Lincoln's wife? Finnola Simms must be old. "Well, I don't really have any favorite celebrities, but I'll be sure to say 'hello' to *your* celebrity crush, Finnola, if I run into her when I'm in Hollywood this weekend."

I said it all casual. Not jealous at all. Really. Not.

"Last I heard she was living in New York City working as a big-time editor, focusing on books about animals."

Ox grinned. "So I doubt either of us will see her."

Too bad, so sad. But the jealous feeling lifted a bit from my brain.

"Well, I'm glad you had a nice surprise," Ox said. "Because if I correctly understood what Cashmere just said, I have to go spend the next period selling homecoming tickets with her and Sydney."

He looked pained. Ox was too nice to say mean things about people, but I was glad he didn't fall for Sydney's tricks to woo him.

"Maybe I can set up a second table across the cafeteria," Ox said. "Far, far on the opposite side. Wish me luck."

I checked myself. Nope, no jealous signals from my brain. I was glad I could trust Ox. Unless that Finnola Sims was around. Grrr—

Ox turned around and smiled at me again as he walked away. He mouthed something at me:

I'll miss you!

I read that loud and clear! Happy sigh. Poor Finnola Sims didn't know what she was missing out on. And now I couldn't waste a moment of thought about it because because I had other things to think about. In the next few hours I had to finish school, tutor Mason and Jason, and pack my suitcase for . . . HOLLYWOOD!

Seven

AFTER SCHOOL, IN BEDROOM

Okay, it was packing time. Packing for my trip to Hollywood! I still couldn't believe it. I felt a little bad for my mom downstairs, who couldn't go because she had to work.

But not so bad that I didn't borrow her turquoise necklace and dangly silver earrings! Hee! I went into my room, carrying the jewels. Now, where to start? Emma was already in there, packing a rolling tote bag with books.

"The important stuff is packed," Emma said, nodding. "Books and study materials. And now I need to pack some clothes."

The doorbell rang and I heard my mom call for me.

"Payton!" she called up. "Nick is here!"

"Nick is here?" I asked. "At our house?"

I looked at Emma and she shrugged.

"I'll pack my stuff and you go see Nick," Emma said. "Now go!"

I went. I raced through the upstairs hall and halfway down the stairs. Then I slowed down and walked casually down the remaining stairs and around the corner to the front hall. Nick was looking very cute in a button-down olive green shirt and jeans.

"Hi, Nick," I said, all calm and casual. It came out more like "Blik, glik."

Nick looked puzzled. I took a deep breath and tried again.

"Hi. Nick," I said carefully, this time actually sounding calm and casual.

"Hey, I didn't get to see you in school, and then I heard you were leaving," Nick said. "I tried texting you but when you didn't answer I thought maybe it would be okay if I stopped by."

He stuck his hands into his pockets and looked uncomfortable.

"Definitely," I said. "My mom took my cell phone away until I was done packing so I wouldn't be distracted.

But I was going to text you when I didn't see you! It was crazy! I found out I'm going to Hollywood, then it's like in five hours and I have to pack and I thought I'd see you in Drama Club and then I came home . . ."

I realized I was babbling so I shut my mouth.

"Anyway, I'm glad you came over," I said.

"Well, I wanted to wish you luck." He smiled. "And tell you that it's awesome that you got cast in that commercial with Emma."

"Thanks," I said. "I'm excited. Okay, and really nervous."

"Of course you're nervous, but you'll be great," he said. "You were a natural on camera in VOGS."

I grinned. That made me feel really good.

"Sometime I want to go out there to LA, maybe work the camera on a TV show or something," he said. "So you'll have to tell me what it's like on a real shoot."

He ran his hand through his wavy brown hair. He looked adorable.

"I will," I said.

"And when you get back, you still want to go to homecoming with me?"

"Definitely," I said. I couldn't wait! Two weeks! My first dance!

We stood there looking at each other. Then he took a deep breath.

"So, maybe this is kind of awkward, but I brought something for you," he said. "Well, not really for you, but kind of for you. . . ."

His voice trailed off as he walked out the front door and then reappeared inside with a guitar strapped onto him.

Nick played guitar? He started strumming. Nick played guitar!

"I wrote this for you," he said.

Nick wrote songs? He wrote songs FOR ME?

Nick played a really pretty song on his guitar and I leaned against the wall in surprise. Oh wow. No guy had ever played a song for me before. Actually, no guys had pretty much ever done anything for me before.

I listened to the music, and notes, and tried to let it sink in that Nick had arranged them! And was playing! A song on the guitar! For me! It was so pretty! It was so sweet! It was so . . . interrupted.

Thump! Thump! Emma came down the stairs, stamping—heavily and loudly—on each step. Nick stopped playing.

"I'm done packing! I'm coming down!" she yelled.

"Downstairs, passing the living room, where I will be able to see and hear people who are in the front hall."

"Emma!" I yelled up to her. "You're interrupting—"

"I don't want to know what I'm interrupting!" she yelled. "TMI! TMI!"

"She means well," I told Nick. "Sorry."

"It's okay," he said. "That was the last part of it."

"I loved it," I said. We smiled at each other.

"Can I help you with your suitcase?" Nick's gaze broke away and he called to Emma.

He was such a gentleman! A nice guy!

"I got it, thanks." Emma made it down to the bottom of the steps and looked at us. "Hey, you have a guitar? I didn't know you played guitar, Nick. That's so cool."

"So was the song he just played me!" I squeaked. "So cool! Thanks, Nick!"

"I guess I should go so you can get ready," Nick said, and we walked to the front door, where he turned to me. "Anyway, so . . ."

We stood there awkwardly, looking at each other. Emma stood there looking at us. I looked at Emma, and she got the hint and went to the kitchen.

"Okay, have fun," he said. "Text me if you get bored."

"I will," I said. "Well, hopefully I won't get bored. But if I do, I'll text you. And if I don't, I'll text you."

Stop babbling, Payton.

Nick leaned over and gave me a hug good-bye. He smelled like grapes, shampoo, and guitar. Then he left.

Squee!

SQUEE!!!!

"Emma!" I accosted her. "Nick just played me a song! It was for ME! Isn't that romantic? I think it's romantic!"

"Did the song go like this? 'Payton and Nick, sitting in a tree, k-i-s-s-'"

"Ag, stop that!" I said. "There was no k-i-s-s-i-n-g! There was a hug, though."

"Romantic, yes," Emma said. "Timely, no. I need to shock you back into reality that we are leaving for the airport early tomorrow, and if I'm not mistaken, you want to wear decent clothes on the trip."

My "squee" turned to "ack!" ACK! I needed to pack!

I raced upstairs into our bedroom and tried to calm my head. I was on total and complete overload. Nick! Hollywood! Nick!

"Very early!" Emma yelled from downstairs, which would have been annoying except that it actually was helpful. Now I needed to focus on Hollywood!

Dad had left my suitcase near my door. I opened it up and saw a bunch of old summer clothes inside that belonged to Emma. She must have forgotten to unpack them from summer camp.

I had no time to unpack the suitcase nicely. I went to Emma's closet, dumped her clothes in, and shut the door. Then I started to pack.

Payton's Packing Process*
- White shirt, big belt, Summer Slave** jeans!
- Cute reddish tee
- Teal dress (so glad I bought the dress for Quinn's bat mitzvah ahead of time! Woot!)
- Black party shoes
- Denim dress
- Denim shorts
- Blue-sequined Summer Slave tank top***
- A bathing suit (maybe there will be a pool . . . or a beach!)
- A second bathing suit (for different days at the pool . . . or beach)

- Purple T-shirt and pj shorts to sleep in
- Cutest flip-flops
- Fuchsia scarf to bring out the color of my cheeks
- Chunky rings, and bracelets, necklaces, and earrings
- And, of course, sunglasses for the California sun!

* Stolen from Ashlynn's Packing Process. Yes, I watched and learned at summer camp.

** Okay, yes, I thought I had retired the Summer Slave clothes, but they needed to make a comeback. They were still the coolest things I owned!

*** Yes, I needed to stop letting Ashlynn pop into my head. She was out of my life—get her out of my head!

Oh yes! Yes, yes, and yes! I was ready to go to . . .
HOLLYWOOD!

Emma

Eight

ON THE PLANE

"I think I see Hollywood!" Payton said.

"For the hundredth time, you just see clouds." I rolled my eyes. "And I know you're just doing it to annoy me so I'll switch seats with you."

Payton stopped leaning on me.

"But I deserve the window seat," she complained. "You're not even looking out. You're doing homework, for Pete's sake."

"Look," I said patiently. "The ticket with my name on it said row 14E. E for the window. E for Emma. You got seat D, the center seat. D for 'drop it.'"

"As if anyone pays attention," my twin said. "No

one would notice—or care—if we changed seats."

"They would if the plane crashed, and only one of us survived, and they identified us by their seating chart," I said.

"I can't believe you just said that," Payton said. "Dad, Emma's talking about the plane crashing."

Our father, who was seated in the aisle seat on my sister's other side, opened his eyes.

"Girls," he said. "This is supposed to be a vacation. I was lucky enough to get the days off from work so your mother could stay home and make her deadline, so no more squabbling."

"Sorry," Payton and I said together.

I went back to writing for a while.

"Payton?" I said. "Remember in New York City, when I got water in my ears from the hotel pool?"

"Sure," Payton said. "You couldn't hear anything. We could have used twin ESP then."

"Well," I said, "People can't learn extrasensory perception, of course, so I was thinking: What could help people who have temporarily lost their hearing?"

Payton yawned.

"Come on," I encouraged. "This could be my groundbreaking science fair project."

"American Sign Language," Payton said. "That's what people who can't hear use."

"Exactly!" I nodded. "Except it's not yet a universally known language. Plus, I tried to learn it, and it didn't work right."

Payton looked at me.

"This is a long trip," she said, "so I'll ask. Emma, why didn't it work?"

"After two hours of trying to learn 'Hello, I'm Emma and I cannot hear right now,' this is what I can do."

I moved my fingers into the positions I'd seen on YouTube.

And watched as Payton collapsed into giggles.

"I know," I said, frustrated. "How can millions of people do this, and I look like my fingers are exploding off my wrists?"

"It's the famous Mills lack of coordination." Payton giggled some more.

It was true. Since middle school had started, there were people who were convinced I had "vestibular," or balance, issues. Just because I seemed to fall. A lot. Loudly. And Payton wasn't much better. We were embarrassing.

"So instead of embarrassing myself," I said, "I switched to language of lip-reading."

 66

"Is that an actual language?" my sister said.

"Not yet," I told her. "But it will be after I present my science fair project titled 'Lip-reading: Efficient and Valuable Communication for the General Population.' And then I can even earn foreign language credits in it toward college! It's win-win!"

"You are weird-weird," Payton pronounced. "But that does remind me, my lips feel chapped. It's really dry in here."

"Oh! The lack of moisture is due to—"

"La la la, not listening. Or lip-reading." Payton was apparently not interested in my scientific expertise anymore.

Fine. I tried to get back to writing, but my sister started pulling things out of her handbag. Lots of things. I stared.

"What? These are youcanbelikeaceleb.com's top must-haves for travel," she said. "A mister for keeping skin dewy, cucumber eye pads to reduce puffiness, wintergreen gum for ear popping and fresh breath . . . hmm . . . Where is my lip hydrator? Dad, wake up!"

"Huh?" Our father opened his eyes. "Are we there?"

"Not yet," Payton told him. "Can you please get my bag down from the overhead compartment? I'm in desperate need of something."

Dad grumbled, but stood up and yanked down a red suitcase.

"No, Dad," I told him. "That's my suitcase. Get the other one."

"No, Dad," Payton said. "You're right. That's my suitcase. Emma's is the other one."

"Girls," Dad said. "The 'other' one is mine. This is the only suitcase you girls brought, and I must say I'm impressed that you packed so well."

"Only one suitcase?" I asked. "Then Payton forgot hers. Because I packed all my stuff in that one."

My sister looked at me.

"Those weren't your old summer clothes being stored in that case?" she asked.

"No, they were my things for California," I said.

"Um, I don't think they'll be in California anytime soon," Payton said slowly. "I left them in a pile in your closet."

"All my clothes?" *My comfy-yet-cute outfits that were totally me?*

"Well, good thing you two are the same size," Dad said, tossing the suitcase back up into the overhead bin. "You'll just have to share."

The itchy-yet-trendy outfits that were totally Payton?.

"But I only have enough for me—on a carefully planned schedule!" my twin whined.

"I don't want to look like Payton," I also whined. Two Paytons walking around in Hollywood? And no Emmas? A totally unfair equation.

"Okay," Dad said. "I'll take you shopping for underwear."

"Dad!" Payton and I both shrieked.

People's heads turned to look at us from all directions.

"Are you girls twins?" an elderly lady asked from one row up, diagonal. "My great-grandsons are twins. Here, let me show you pictures. . . ."

I smiled weakly as Dad started talking to her.

"I'll trade you the window seat for the first wearing of your teal dress," I whispered. I'd worn it once during a twin switch, so at least I knew it was not too itchy.

"Deal," Payton said.

We switched places.

"Our first twin switch in midair," my sister said, as I climbed over and she scooched under.

I couldn't help but smile.

"Very funny," I said.

"I think I see Hollywood!" Payton said, looking out the window.

Whatever.

Ding! The FASTEN SEAT BELT sign lit up over our heads.

"Ladies and gentlemen," the pilot announced, "we are now beginning our descent. The weather in Los Angeles is a balmy eighty degrees and sunny."

I couldn't help it. I leaned over on top of Payton to look out the window.

I saw land! I saw land!

Payton and I looked at each other. OMGosh!

"Read my lips," Payton whispered, and mouthed something.

I translated that one easily, even through her chapped lips:

Squeeeeee!

Nine

HOLLYWOOD!!!

Ahhhhh . . . Los Angeles, California! The palm trees were so tall—according to Emma, more than one hundred feet tall. Tall, tall trees with a burst of leaves at the top! It was sunny and warm and you could see mountains in the background and the whole drive from the airport we were screaming, AAHHHH!!! We were in Hollywood!

I had expected that we would stay in a hotel like the one in New York City. Here in LA, apparently, things would be a little different. Instead of a tiny room in a very tall building, we were staying in an apartment in a complex of short buildings.

But I certainly wasn't complaining. We walked in the door and looked at each other.

"It's huge!" I gasped.

"It has a kitchen and a living room and a desk area!" Emma clapped her hands. "And I call the desk area!"

"Nice crib," my Dad said approvingly. "'Crib' is Hollywood-speak, right? Or should I say, nice pad?"

"Stick with crib, Dad," I advised him, cracking up.

Emma immediately unzipped her laptop case, put her laptop on the desk, and started muttering about wi-fi. I continued my tour of the apartment.

"Three bedrooms!" I squealed. "We'll each have our own room!"

Emma and I have always shared a room. At home, on vacation, in New York City . . . but not in Hollywood! For the first time in my life I wouldn't have to hear Emma complaining about my mess and me responding she must have sucked up all the organization genes. For the first time in my life I wouldn't have to hear Emma talking in her sleep. Sure, I probably actually learned something from Emma mumbling math calculations and spelling out long words, but for the next two nights I could have a quiet, genius-free sleep!

Woo-hoo!

Emma was still frowning as she adjusted her Internet access, so I took full advantage and ran around to see the bedrooms. They were all painted white and had tan carpeting and pictures of flowers in vases on the walls. One was obviously the master bedroom and there were two smaller ones. One smaller one had two twin-size beds and overlooked a beautiful view of the mountains. The other one had a big bed and a TV but a teeny closet space. They were connected by a shared bathroom. Hmm.

"Dad, you probably want the big one," I whispered to him so Emma wouldn't catch on that I was about to choose a bedroom. "So may I choose my room?"

"Sure," Dad said. "But I don't need the big room. You girls can decide."

Seriously?

"Dibs on the big bedroom!" I yelled, racing into the master bedroom. Wowza, it had two huge beds! Its own bathroom! A hot tub! A walk-in closet! I went into the closet and pictured where I'd put all my stuff. I stepped outside the closet and looked around. This was going to be great! This was going to be—

"Excuse me," Emma said, pushing the bedroom door open and entering the room. And not only entering it, but also dragging my suitcase.

"Oh, thank you!" I said. "That's so nice of you to bring the suitcase to my room for me."

"Your room?" Emma sniffed. "I don't think so. I want this room. Dad said I could have it. I figured we could put all the clothes in the big closet and—"

"What?!" I shrieked. "I called dibs!"

"Dad beats dibs," Emma said calmly. "I said I would like it, he said it was fine with him. This will be the perfect room for me to spread out all of my flash cards. And tons of floor space as I recite my spelling words for the next competition."

Emma held up her flash cards and started flashing them at herself while pacing the length of the room, chanting words that sounded inhuman.

"That's not fair!" I said to her. "This will be the perfect room for me to lay out all of our potential outfits to wear to the set, and then there's the fact that you don't take bubble baths. It would be a waste of the hot tub."

She was ignoring me! I would not be ignored.

"Cat! K-a-t!" I shouted. "Dog! D-a-w-g!"

I jumped in front of Emma and waved my hands around. She tried to act like I wasn't distracting her and continued calculating loudly.

"From the Latin, which means . . . ," Emma went on.

"From the Pig Latin, which means . . ." My efforts were futile. Man, my twin had focus. I climbed up onto one of the beds and started jumping on it. Ooh, it was so fluffy and bouncy and huge. Now I was even more determined to get this room. I would have to get in her face so she couldn't ignore me anymore.

"This room is mine!" I yelled and launched myself off the bed so that I flew through the air and landed directly in front of her. Or that was the plan, anyway.

OOF! and *BAM!*

Instead I landed directly on my twin. I knocked her over and we both plunged to the floor under a cascade of flying flash cards. I hit my knee on Emma's skull, and she bonked her elbow into my stomach.

"Ow!" We both yelled at exactly the same time. Then we both yelled louder. "OW!"

"What is going on in here?" The door flew open and my father stood there with his arms crossed. He looked down and saw us in a heap on the floor.

"She started it!" we both yelled, pointing at each other.

"She jumped off the bed and attacked me!" Emma said, rubbing her head.

"She stole my bedroom!" I said, rubbing my stomach.

"It's my bedroom. Daddy said," Emma said.

"I can see my efforts in trying to be nice and giving up the big bedroom were a mistake," my father said. "I thought you two had worked it out. I should have put you each in one of the smaller bedrooms I see."

"But this bedroom is perfect for my studying," Emma protested.

"But it's perfect for my fashion planning for the commercial," I said. "Plus I'm the one who brought bubble bath—perfect for the Jacuzzi tub of awesome."

Emma and I glared at each other and waited for Dad to make his decision.

"Sounds like the bedroom is perfect for . . ." He paused. We held our breath. ". . . both of you to share."

"What?" we both said.

"But there are three bedrooms!" Emma said. "Three people, three bedrooms. Even Payton can do that math."

I shot her a look.

"This trip to Hollywood should bring you closer," Dad said. "You two have to work as a team. Sharing a room will make sure of it."

"But—" we both protested. Then stopped when we saw our dad's face turn serious.

"I will chalk this little incident up to jet lag," he said.

"Or tween hormones. Your mother did give me a little book on puberty to read. Maybe I should read it on the set while you're filming—"

Emma and I gave each other looks of panic. Dad reading a puberty book on our set?

"Ack, no!" I cut him off. "It was definitely jet lag!"

"Yes, jet lag can cause disorientation, lack of judgment, irritability, and other behaviors that are not hormonally related!" Emma added. "In summary, we're fine with sharing a room. No problem."

"And maybe you should just give us the book about um, puberty." I mumbled the last word. "Emma probably wants to read it tonight before bed."

Emma shot me a look.

We don't want him to bring it to the set! I mouthed to her. *Embarrassing!*

She lip-read that and nodded.

"All good." I pushed Dad out of the room. "We need girl time to unpack now."

"And I'll set up my room. Rooms!" Dad's mood lightened up. "I've always dreamed of a man cave. I'll use one of the bedrooms to sleep and the big one to watch sports and eat chips and get crumbs everywhere and your mom can't scold me. This works out fantastic!"

He walked out of the room and we heard him let out a "Woo-hoo!"

"Yeah, woo and who." I sighed, shutting the door to our bedroom. Emphasis on the *our*.

"Good job, Payton," Emma said. "Now we have to share a room. I was so looking forward to a room that was perfectly spotless and organized."

"Well, since we only brought my clothes, we won't have too much that can make a mess," I told her.

"And for once I thought I could have my own bedroom so I wouldn't have to hear you sleep-talk at night." Emma sighed.

Wait, what?

"I sleep-talk? You never told me that!"

"I guess I thought you knew," Emma said. "Every night you mumble about Nick. Like once you said his ankles were so cute . . ."

"Ack!" I shrieked, flinging myself onto one of the beds (the bed closest to the window with a great view). "I do? I do *not*. I don't, do I?"

"No, you don't. I was just kidding," Emma said, smiling.

I threw a pillow at her. And missed.

"And don't think I don't realize you flung yourself

78

on that bed and messed it up so you could claim it."

"I deserve the choice of bed after you tortured me with the sleep-talking comment," I said.

"That's fine," Emma replied, sitting down on the other one. "This bed is on the side of the room with more floor space. Plus, I owe you for getting that book away from Dad. I've heard stage parents can be embarrassing, but that would be really humiliating if he read a book about puberty on the set."

"Agreed," I said. "How about I unpack and you can use the time to study your flash cards?"

"That sounds deceptively generous. Is this a ploy to keep me away from your clothes for as long as possible?" Emma squinted at me.

"Yes." I laughed. "Although I have to admit, with your new fashion sense, I wouldn't mind a second opinion on what outfits we should wear to the set tomorrow."

"*Fashion Passion* magazine says chili-pepper red is going to trend," Emma suggested. "While I'm not sure if they mean ripe extra-spicy chili pepper or the miniature lighter-colored variety, your red shirt is probably close."

I smiled and pulled out a reddish shirt. I was hanging up our clothes in the closet and ignoring Emma chanting math facts when there was a knock on the door.

"Are you ready to explore outside?" Dad asked.

"Yes," I said. "And so is Emma."

"May I bring my flash cards?" Emma asked. I answered her by grabbing her flash cards from her hands and tossing them on her bed. Emma sighed and we both followed Dad out the door.

"I think there's a pool," Dad said.

"Oh, there's more than one pool. I informed you both of that." Emma put her hands on her hips. "Didn't you two read the article I e-mailed you about this place?"

Dad and I looked at each other guiltily. Emma forwarded me about fifty e-mails a day with things she thought I should read, including scientific articles and financial columns. Other than the cute YouTube videos with babies and kittens, I just clicked delete. I could tell by the look on Dad's face he pretty much did the same thing.

"So you don't know that we have two pools at this complex," Emma said. "Does that mean you don't know anything about this place? Do you know who stays here?"

"What do you mean 'who stays here'?" I asked.

And that's when Emma explained more about the apartment complex. It was a common place for kids who want to break into show business—or who already are in show business—to stay if they don't live in Los Angeles.

"So other kids like us who are filming, or kids who are auditioning, are staying here," Emma finished.

"So right now some stars may be living here?" That was so cool!

Emma nodded.

"This might be your only chance to swim," Dad said. "I just got a text that your script will be delivered later this afternoon and you have tonight to learn your lines. Why don't you two change into your bathing suits?"

Script! Lines! I suddenly felt nervous and pressured. I definitely needed to take my mind off of that!

And a pool full of possible celebrities was just what I needed.

Ten

A HOLLYWOOD POOL

Payton and I changed into our bathing suits. Well, into Payton's bathing suits. It had been fortuitous on her part to pack two suits. Payton wore an orange suit with gold buckles and I had a nautical flavor in navy blue stripes. We both put on our sunglasses.

"Ready, girls?" Our dad looked ready to relax in a Hawaiian shirt and a white sunscreen blotch on his nose.

We walked outside and passed tennis courts and a little grocery store. We went into the pool area, where people were lounging on beach chairs and swimming around the pool.

"Emma," Payton said quietly to me. "Are you really in the mood to go swimming? I feel out of place. It's so glamorous."

"Well, I was really in the mood to continue studying calculus with my flash cards," I replied. "But since you dragged me here, yes. Let's swim. I can practice some moves for water polo."

Dad put his towel down on one chair and Emma and I walked to a different row of chairs and put our stuff down. No offense, Dad.

"There might be real, live stars in the pool." Payton scanned the area. "Or future ones."

"Like you, Actress Twin," I told her. My twin gets intimidated easily. I do not, having honed my confidence through competitions where others would be intimi dated for example the Math Olympics, when I went mano a mano against state-ranked Hannah "Human Calculator" Jones.

I also did not get starstruck.

"Stars are just people too," I told Payton.

The pool was full of people playing with beach balls and swimming around. Payton walked up to the edge, but then lost her nerve and went to the empty hot tub.

"Let's warm up in here," Payton suggested.

"But then we'll freeze later," I pointed out. "Our body temperature will rise but then—"

Payton ignored me and slid into the hot tub. I went over and stuck my toe in.

"Ouch hot hot," I said. Ooch.

"Come on in, it's so relaxing," Payton said. "I want to relax now while I have the chance. Can you believe we have a commercial shoot tomorrow?"

Before I could answer I heard a voice speak.

"You guys have a commercial shoot tomorrow?" I turned to see a girl standing behind me. She was tall and tanned, in a silver bikini and aviator sunglasses.

"Oh sorry, I hope I'm not interrupting a private conversation," she said. "Mind if I join you?"

"Sure!" Payton said. I could tell she was happy that someone here was friendly.

"I'm Jessica," she said. "Are you guys new here?"

"We just got here," Payton said. "I'm Payton and that's Emma. I love your sunglasses."

"I'm guessing you guys are twins," Jessica said, sitting down and dangling her feet into the hot tub. "I'm a twin too."

"Cool!" Payton said. I felt weird being the only one standing up, so I succumbed to peer pressure, ignored my own advice about body temperature, and gingerly slid into the hot tub. Okay, kind of nice. "Are you guys identical or fraternal?" This was usually the first question people asked us, and that other twins asked each other.

"Fraternal," Jessica said. "We're *nothing* alike. I'm tall, she's short. My hair is obviously black and straight, hers is shorter and red and curly."

I relaxed into the bubbles and thought for a second how much different it would be if Payton and I were fraternal. What if, for example, she had shorter red curly hair and I had black straight hair? Or if she was very short and I was very tall? Or if I had been a boy? Named Peyton! The genetic combinations and permutations were mind-boggling, even for a mathlete.

"It's cooler to be identical," Jessica said. "People always look at us and are like: really? You're sure you're twins? You're *nothing* alike."

"There are pros and cons," I mused. "Nobody mixes you up. Nobody calls you clones."

"Nobody analyzes how your nose is bigger than your twin's," Payton pointed out.

"Yeah, but people say things like: Oh, your twin is so lucky to have that gorgeous red hair, like I'm supposed to feel like I got gypped or something," Jessica said. "Or they ask her when she's going to grow so she doesn't look like my little sister."

Yes, being fraternal would present its own set of challenges. I decided both situations had their advantages and disadvantages.

"Identical twin babies are a Hollywood score," Jessica continued. "Too bad for you your parents didn't bring you out here at birth. They always need identical baby twins to play one character," Jessica said. "You guys could have been hired as babies. You could be superstars, billionaires, and own your own fashion line by now."

I wondered what I would have been like as a baby actor. On one hand, I would have been great with a script, given the exceptionally early age I began to read. On the other hand, I did not like to smile or giggle on cue like the baby actors I saw on television. My favorite toy had been a chess set.

Payton probably would have been a great baby actor. My mom said if you held up something shiny or sparkly in front of her, she would smile and coo.

Like she was cooing now.

"So you know a lot about Hollywood? Are you an actor?" Payton cooed.

"Who isn't, around here?" Jessica said. "Or a wannabe.

So are you guys auditioning for the commercial or have you already been cast?

"We've already been cast," Payton said.

"It's our first commercial," I said. "Actually it's pretty much a first anything, including our first time in LA."

I ignored Payton's look. I could tell she thought I was making us sound less cool to Jessica. Unlike us, Jessica looked like a star, and Payton wanted to impress her. She had done that with Sydney, though, and look where that got us. Into double trouble.

"Wow, that's a big deal," Jessica said. "A commercial on your first trip here? A lot of people come here a bunch of times hoping for any kind of gig. So what kind of commercial?"

"It's for shampoo," I told her. I tried to shake out my hair a little so that it would shine in the sun and look like the kind of hair that could be in a commercial. I did have my pride. I noticed out of the corner of my eye that Payton was doing the same thing.

Jessica looked at both of us.

"Oh, that's totally cool," she said. "What shampoo?"

"It's called Teen Sheen," Payton said.

"Nice," she said. Then she looked up and her expression darkened. "Oh, hello."

I looked over and saw another girl. She was tall with freckled skin and had short, curly red hair. I surmised she was Jessica's twin.

"Really, Jessica?" she asked. "They've only been here about three minutes. That must be a record for you."

"I was just being friendly." Jessica smiled. But she pulled herself out of the hot tub and grabbed her towel. "Must go! Buh-bye!"

She quickly walked away.

"Sorry about my twin," the girl said.

"Sorry about what?" Payton asked. "She was just being friendly."

"Was she asking friendly questions about whether or not you had any auditions? Or who your agent is?" the girl asked.

Payton and I looked at each other.

"She did ask about a commercial we're here to film," I admitted.

"Did you tell her anything?" the girl asked, then shook her head when Emma and I nodded. "Well, I'm sure it won't mean anything. But Jessica is kind of a shark. She looks for new people and sees if they have any useful information."

"Ah," I said. I got it. "Such as where auditions are

or perhaps who is filming commercials. So she can try to steal the audition or role."

I had dealt with this at competitions, where people would try to sneak looks at your study material or find out your special tricks! I should have smelled that one coming a mile away.

"Don't be embarrassed," the girl said. "Rookie mistake. You might want to be cautious about what you tell people, that's all. It's pretty competitive around here!"

"Okay, thanks," Payton mumbled.

"I'm Shira, by the way," the girl said. "The non-shark twin."

"And what do you want?" I asked Shira suspiciously.

"Nothing." Shira laughed. "We've lived here almost a year while Jessica tries for her big break, so I've seen it all."

I looked at her and raised an eyebrow.

"Honest." Shira smiled. "Though, full disclosure, I would love to be an actress, but, well, it's tricky. Anyway, just to be helpful again—I think you got a script or something."

"How do you know?"

"Is that your manager? Your dad?" she pointed at our dad.

Payton and I both swiveled our heads to look at our

father. He was sitting on a beach chair, signing a package from a delivery person.

"Our dad," I said.

"The way Jessica is sniffing around his chair, I bet the package has a script or something to do with your commercial," Shira said.

Our lines! It must be our lines! Payton and I looked at each other and immediately jumped out of the hot tub.

"Thanks!" I told Shira. I noticed that Jessica had gotten close enough to read what Dad was looking at. He was oblivious to the girl peering over his shoulder.

I had to intercept this. It was like the time at Science Olympiad when I computed the trajectory of an airborne object in motion along with the force of gravity to determine its point of collision. I reached down and picked up one of the beach balls at the side of the pool. I tossed it in the air and, using one of my water-polo moves I'd been practicing, I bopped it over and . . .

Smack!

Hit the ball. It soared through the air and hit Jessica right in the shoulder, knocking her off-balance. Dad looked up, closed the paper, and asked if she was okay.

She was fine, but foiled. Ha! A perfect hit!

Score one for Emma! (And physics and calculus!)

Payton

Eleven

IN A BLACK CAR WITH TINTED WINDOWS, ROLLING THROUGH HOLLYWOOD

I had practiced our lines over and over all night and now in the car on the way to the studio.

"Oh, my hair!" I said.

And:

"I love having shiny hair. Shiny hair makes me feel shiny inside."

And:

"Shiny *and* shiny! Double the shiny!"

Okay, yes they were dorky. But I was trying to ignore that. Twin #1 would say the first line and Twin #2 would say the second one. We'd say the third line together. We didn't know which one of us would be Twin #1 or #2.

Of course, Emma hoped she'd be Twin #1, since she wants to be number one at everything.

After we say those lines, we're supposed to swish our shiny hair. *Swish, swish.*

"Can you please stop that," Emma complained from the seat next to me. "You're hitting me with one swish and Dad with the other."

"Oh sorry," I apologized. "Just rehearsing."

I swished one last time and my white sunglasses flew off my face and landed on the floor of the car by Emma's feet. I gave her an apologetic look. Oopsie.

"Don't make yourself dizzy." Dad smiled. "We're almost there."

I leaned back in the comfortable leather seats. The studio had sent a car to pick us up, which meant we had our own car and driver! I had felt like a movie star this morning when the black car pulled up in front of our apartment. I had hoped Jessica was watching and thinking, *Oh those twins are superstars in their fancy car.*

I closed my eyes and pretended I was a real TV star with my own personal chauffeur, pulling up to a Hollywood premiere. The car would stop and I'd step out, wearing superspiky high platform heels (And I didn't even fall. Hey, it was my daydream!) I'd step out and flashbulbs would pop in front of my eyes and the paparazzi would yell, "Payton! Payton!"

"Payton! Payton!"

I opened my eyes. It wasn't the paparazzi; it was my sister. We had arrived at the studio!

I had pictured a studio, like one room, but it turned out the place was a bunch of studios and offices, and it was huge. We had to walk through a maze of buildings to get to Studio 7.

I was so nervous as we got checked in and taken to the place where we'd film the commercial. I could tell Emma was nervous too, because she kept muttering, "Shiny *and* shiny! Double the shiny!" under her breath. In a blur, we were signed in, greeted, and whisked off to a room. We were introduced to the assistant director. That's AD in Hollywood-speak. (Hee! Hollywood-speak!)

And the AD asked us *the* twin question. The question we'd heard all of our lives:

"Which one are you?"

And as always, Emma answered for us.

"I'm Emma," she said. "And she's Payton."

But the AD smiled and shook her head.

"Actually what I was asking was, which one of you is Twin Number One and which is Twin Number Two?"

Emma and I looked at each other, stumped.

"Nobody told us," I said.

"We each have both parts memorized," Emma added. "So we're ready either way."

"Well, let's figure it out now. You might not realize it from the lines, but one role requires a little bit more emotional range," the AD said.

"I'll do it!" More emotion! More range! More acting! I jumped at that.

"Okay, Payton is Twin Number One," she said.

I saw Emma bite her lip and control herself. I knew she wanted to say she would be Twin #1. Any chance Emma had to be number one, she had a compulsive need to take it. I thought about switching. But nah. I wanted the emotional range. Plus, hee hee! I would get to taunt Emma, which I did when the AD went to find out where we were supposed to be next.

"I'm number one," I sang out. "You're number two. NUMBER TWO. Heh-heh."

"Very mature," Emma said. "I thought I'd left Mason back home."

I was still smiling when the AD came back with the plan. First we would have some fittings and stylings, then we'd go to the set for rehearsal. Fittings and stylings!

"Twin Number One, you'll need extra time in the hairstylist chair." She glanced at me.

Squee! I was going to get extra hairstyling! Maybe I was having my straight hair curled into beachy waves. Or glamorous curls. It was awesome being Twin #1!

"And then, wardrobe."

Squee, squee, double the squee! I wondered what I would be wearing. I hoped it would be a fantasy sequence, where I'd be wearing a long dress and perhaps a tiara on my shiny hair. Or a supertrendy outfit with really cool boots. Maybe tall black boots. Or—

Emma was told to go to her wardrobe fitting. Wardrobe fitting was awesome, too! I saw Emma smile a little. She used to hate anything fashiony, but ever since our twin switch at the mall she had a new appreciation for style.

"Bye, Emma!" I waved. She turned and smiled and I mouthed, *Bye, number two!* Hee hee, I couldn't resist. I went to the hairstylist's chair and she introduced herself as Jean-Marie. She had short, spiky brown hair and dramatic eye makeup.

"Since this is a hair commercial, obviously getting the hair exactly right is crucial," Jean-Marie said, examining strands of my hair. "Crucial!"

"Oh yes," I told her. "Definitely *crucial*!"

"Your hair is perfect for my plan," she cooed.

Yay! My hair was Hollywood-perfect! Wait until I told Emma, the 'shinier' hair twin. While Jean-Marie was putting some kind of oily gel in my hair, to make it shinier and silkier I guess, Emma came back in. I almost fell off my chair.

Emma was wearing a bright royal blue T-shirt with fuchsia-colored tank top straps peeking out of the top and a yellow skirt.

"You look so colorful!" I said. Emma usually wore muted colors, or serious colors. This outfit made her skin look rosier, her eyes pop.

"I do." Emma shifted uncomfortably. "It's not exactly me."

"That's part of acting," I said. "Assuming other personas, becoming comfortable in their skin. Dealing with what the hair and makeup people think is best for the role."

"Very true," Jean-Marie said. And then she straightened up and spun my chair toward the mirror.

"Twin Number One, you are ready to go," she announced.

I looked at my reflection in the mirror. I could see Emma standing behind me looking at my reflection in the mirror. This time we didn't look identical, thanks to my hair. Emma looked at me and my hair and shot me a puzzled look. I shot her a puzzled look back.

I still had a head full of oily slickness.

"Um," I said. "I'm done . . . how? I'm all greasy!"

"I know, it's perfect isn't it!" Jean-Marie smiled. "It should stay that way all day and then we'll regrease tomorrow."

All day? Regrease?

"You are Twin Number One, right?" Jean-Marie looked momentarily concerned.

"Yes," I replied.

"*Ohhh . . . ,*" Jean-Marie said. "Is this is a surprise to you? Didn't you get the script?"

"My script says, 'Shiny *and* shiny! Double the shiny!'" I said. "Not greasy *and* greasy! Double the greasy."

"Those are your lines." She nodded. "But my instructions are that Twin Number One is the twin who doesn't use Teen Sheen. Greasy gross hair for scene one."

Greasy gross hair for . . . Oh, crumbcakes.

"Ha-ha!" Emma laughed so hard she snorted. "Sorry, Twin Number One!"

"Twin Number Two, since you *do* use the product, we'll make your hair shiny and luxurious," the stylist said.

"My hair is going to look like this the whole commercial?" I gasped.

"No, you'll have shiny hair at the end," the stylist said. "It will just be greasy for most of it."

Agh! Agh!

"I'm *number two*!" Emma did a little shimmy.

"But *I'm* the twin who cares about her appearance," I blurted out. Emma sometimes lets her (I admit, very shiny) hair get a little greasy when she was superstudying for a competition. But I always washed my hair! I would never be seen in public with greasy hair!

"That's part of acting," Emma said, grinning. "Dealing with what hair and makeup think is best for the role. My twin sister told me that advice."

It got worse when I went into wardrobe. I sounded so glam, "going into wardrobe." I came out not so glam.

My outfit was a green T-shirt and gray sweatpants. I looked at myself in the mirror. I looked like I hadn't showered or changed my clothes in days.

"Perfect," said the wardrobe stylist. "You look like you haven't showered or changed your clothes in days."

Sigh. I tried to thank her cheerfully. That really put my acting skills to work. I felt a little crabby and asked to go to the bathroom.

"Don't touch the hair!" someone called to me. Oh, no worries about that. My national television debut and I was greasy! Oily! And pretty much disgusting! I was muttering to myself as I left the room and—

CRASH!

I crashed right into someone. And I couldn't believe who that someone was: Ashlynn.

Ashlynn? Ashlynn from my bunk in summer camp? The girl who called me Summer Slave all summer as I did chores in exchange for her clothes? Ashlynn who was in the off-Broadway show in New York City and tried to embarrass me and my whole Drama Club onstage? (Fail, ha!) Ashlynn, who was looking at me and . . . laughing?

"(A), What are you doing here?" Ashlynn said, hands on her hips. "And (B), Wow, you've gone downhill."

She looked me up and down and smirked.

I was so shocked, I couldn't speak. What was Ashlynn doing here? And why was she here when I was so very, very gross!?

"It reminds me of those three days at camp when the showers went out," she continued. "Of course, I talked my way into using the camp director's shower but you were so dirty and gross."

"Wh-what're you doing here?" I managed to stammer.

"I'm here shooting a shampoo commercial," Ashlynn said, playing with strands of her (shiny!) long honey-blond hair. "My off-Broadway producer Jane's college friend selected me to be in the commercial."

Oh no! Mrs. Burkle's friend recommended Ashlynn, too? She *was* supertalented, superpretty, and superstar material, I had to admit. And supermean.

"Are you in the Teen Sheen commercial?" I asked. *Please say no. Please say no. Pleasesayno—*

"Yes," she said.

Crumbcakes.

"I am too," I said. "That's why my hair is—"

"Nice try," she said. "It's nice that they let tourists in to tour, though, and even talk to the talent. Like *moi*!"

"But—" I tried to cut in but she kept going.

"This has been a lovely surprise, but I have to go to wardrobe," she said. Then she got that wicked grin on her face. "Maybe I can ask them to make you my assistant and you can do my laundry again. You can be my Studio Slave. Get, it? Summer Slave? Isn't that hilarious, Payton?"

Ag! Summer Slave memories flashed up at me again and I panicked. I said the only thing I could think of.

"I'm not Payton. I'm Emma."

Emma

Twelve

STUDIO 7

"Summer Camp-slash-Off-Broadway-Diva Ashlynn?" I said, shocked. That was highly unexpected and unwelcome news.

"And she's in the Teen Sheen commercial too," Payton groaned. "It's not as coincidental as it sounds. Jane recommended her. Fortunately she doesn't have any scenes with us, so hopefully she'll be on a different schedule. But still. She's here."

I frowned.

"And you said you were me?" I asked her.

"Yes. I panicked. It was the only thing I could think of. I choked, I'm sorry." Payton looked down at the floor.

"But we totally took care of her in New York City! You're not supposed to fear Ashlynn," I scolded her.

"I know, I know," Payton moaned. "She said all the exact things to make me feel stupid and there I was in my greasy hair and sweats. I tried to tell her it was for the commercial too, but she didn't believe me."

I looked around the room we were waiting in until we were supposed to rehearse the commercial. Dad was happily enjoying what the crew called "craft services." That meant a big buffet table full of snacks.

"Well." I shrugged. "So be it. If we see Ashlynn again, I'll just go along with it."

"You're the best!" Payton said.

"Happy to help," I said. "Now, if Ashlynn is going to be around we need to pump up your confidence. Remember how we bested her in NYC. And now you're in the commercial, so stop feeling insecure."

"Okay," Payton said in a small voice. Then she cleared her throat. "Okay! I will!"

"And if she bothers you or distracts you during the commercial, how about I do this to help you focus?" I suggested. I moved my lips did some flicking motions with my hands in the air.

"Uh, what are you doing?" Payton asked.

"Lip-singing 'Twinkle, Twinkle, Little Star,' of course," I said. "I know you don't have my mad lip-reading skills, but didn't you catch my twinkling hands? To remind you that you're a star? And of the 'twin' in 'twinkle'?"

"Yes, well, um," Payton said. "Maybe I won't be needing that."

"Good! I knew you could put your past behind you!" I pep-talked. "Yay, Payton."

And then it was time for rehearsal. Of course I knew my lines backward and forward: "I discovered the greatest shampoo. Shampoo greatest the discovered I."

See? Totally ready for this. But I was worried about my sister. That Ashlynn really shakes up her confidence.

"Payton! Emma!"

We got called to the set! When we got there, I surveyed my environment. It looked like a family room, except the walls were fake and in the middle of a studio. There was a tan couch, a matching chair, and peach throw pillows. The walls were painted cream. I was certainly a vivid display of color amidst the muted nature of the scene.

Also adding some color were the crew members who were all over—the cameraperson with a giant camera on wheels, the lighting person adjusting giant lights, a sound person moving a boom microphone around. It was a busy scene.

"Hello! I'm Lewis, the director." A man came over to us. "I'm Bertha Burkle's buddy, and we're happy to have you joining us today. I so enjoyed the video of your being frogs and jumping to and fro, confusing the audience."

He stopped and looked at me. Then Payton.

"Zounds. You *are* identical." He grinned. "That's rad."

And he handed us a fresh copy of the script.

"There are a couple new lines," he said. "See if you can memorize them now. If not, we'll remind you just before you go on. No worries."

SCRIPT: SCENE 1
VOICE-OVER ANNOUNCER: These twins
    are so identical that it's usually hard
    to tell them apart. Until they didn't
    use identical shampoos.
(Twin #1 shakes her head of limp, greasy
    hair and frowns. Twin #2 smiles and
    shakes her head of shiny, fabulous
    hair in slow motion).
TWIN #1: Wow! (gasps) How did you get
    that shiny hair?

TWIN #2: I discovered the greatest new
    shampoo. (Holds up shampoo bottle)
(Twin #1 runs her fingers through her
    oily hair and frowns.)
TWIN #1: "Teen Sheen shampoo? That's
    what made your hair so supershiny?"
(TWIN #2 nods and tosses shampoo
    bottle to Twin #1, who catches it.)

"That's your first scene to shoot today," Lewis said to us. "Are you ready?"

"Yes!" Payton and I said exactly the same time, making some of the crew chuckle.

Payton and I took our places. The AD gave me the shampoo bottle I would be holding up.

"It's so light," I said. I tossed it from hand to hand.

"It's a fake inflatable one." The AD said. "Looks real, doesn't it? But it will be easier for you to toss it to your sister and it'll have a floating quality."

I squeezed the shampoo bottle a little bit. It felt light and squishy, like a blow-up beach ball.

"Through the magic of television it will look solid and real." The AD smiled.

"Places, everyone!" the director said. "Quiet on the set!"

I looked around at all of the crew on the set and the cameras aimed at me and my sister. This was it. We were about to start filming a real, live commercial. Payton and I looked at each other nervously. She mouthed to me, *Break an egg.* I took a wild guess she was telling me to "Break a leg." Actor-speak.

The AD held up a clapboard that said TEEN SHEEN, SCENE ONE, TAKE ONE and snapped it shut with a *clap!*

"And, action!" the director said.

The announcer began: These twins are so identical that it's usually hard to tell them apart. Until they didn't use identical shampoos.

Payton shook her head full of limp, greasy hair and frowned. I smiled and shook my head of shiny, fabulous hair.

Payton gasped and said her first line: "How did you—"

"Cut!" The director yelled.

Payton and I looked at each other with alarm.

"Nice start, twins," the director said. "I think we need the camera to shoot closer, however."

Payton and I both exhaled. Whew, we didn't do anything wrong.

"Teen Sheen, scene one, take two!" the AD said and clapped the board in front of us.

Voice-over Announcer: "*These twins are so identical that it's usually hard to tell them apart. Until they didn't use identical shampoos.*"

Payton shook her head full of oily, greasy hair and frowned. *Ew.* It really was greasy and gross, leaving a trail of goo on her cheeks. Poor Twin #1! I smiled and shook my head of shiny, fabulous hair.

"How did you get that shiny hair?" Payton asked me. And then she gasped.

"I discovered the greatest new shampoo." I smiled and held up the bottle. Out of the corner of my eye I saw Ashlynn walk up to the side of the set. I hoped Payton didn't notice her.

Payton ran her hands through her oily, limp hair, and that's when she glanced over and saw Ashlynn. She visibly flinched.

"Cut!" the director said. "Twin Number One, you looked distracted. Plus, Makeup! Get the greasy streaks off her cheek; they're reflective on camera. Also Twin Number One, don't whip your hair so much."

I could see Payton turn pink, and I saw Ashlynn smirk.

"No worries," the director said to me. "We always do multiple takes to get it just right."

"Don't worry," I reassured my twin quietly. "And do not let Ashlynn distract you. Focus."

"Twin Number One, let me grease your hair a bit," Jean-Marie called out to Payton.

"Twin Number Two, let me brush your hair a bit," the makeup artist called out. I went over and stood still while I was attacked by a hard brush. I watched as Ashlynn sidled over to Payton.

"Well, I wouldn't have believed it if I hadn't seen it with my own eyes," I heard Ashlynn say to Payton. "You twins really are in the commercial."

Payton closed her eyes as she was greased up.

"I'm shooting my big scenes right after you guys," Ashlynn continued. "Although it looks like it could be a while until they get you to do it right."

I tried to send psychic twin messages to my sister: *Ignore, ignore! Ignore Ashlynn!*

"I have to admit I was really surprised to find out that you guys were cast in the commercial," Ashlynn said. "But then I realized it made sense. They needed someone with naturally greasy hair, someone who doesn't care about their hair, someone like you, Emma."

Oh, ouch. Ashlynn still thought that was me. I opened my mouth to defend myself—and Payton, of course—but the makeup artist started wiping off my lipstick with a baby wipe and all I called out was:

"Mmmf! Mmmf!"

Ashlynn and Payton looked over at me.

"Let me just reapply your lip color," the makeup artist said. "And you'll be good to go, Emma."

"Oh, that's not Emma," Ashlynn called over. "It's Payton."

I saw Payton's stricken look. Now she'd have to confess she was the greasy twin. I felt bad for her. I kept my mouth shut as the makeup artist brushed lipstick and sticky gloss on my mouth.

"I thought Payton was Twin Number One." The makeup artist looked rightfully confused.

I waited for Payton to set her straight but Payton looked frozen. Before either of us could say anything, the director called us back to the set.

"We can deal with Ashlynn later," I said quietly to my sister. "Don't let her interfere with your work. You know she just likes to press your buttons for her own entertainment."

"You're right," Payton said. "I won't let her interfere with our acting job. Absolutely not."

Good.

We got back in position for the commercial.

"Teen Sheen scene, take three!" the AD said, doing the clapboard thing.

Voice-over Announcer: "These twins are so identical that it's usually hard to tell them apart. Until they didn't use identical shampoos."

Payton shook her head of limp, greasy hair and frowned. I shook my clean, shiny hair and grinned.

"Cut!" The director said. "Emma, I want to see a smile like you mean it. A *dazzling* smile. Dazzle me, Emma."

"Excuse me!" Ashlynn suddenly called out. Everyone looked at her. "I'm so sorry to interrupt, but it's important. I'm sure the twins don't want to call attention to a mistake, but the twin with the gross, greasy, oily hair is Emma, not Payton."

And the girl over there is extremely annoying, I wanted to say. But I was a professional. Still, I lost any traces of a dazzling smile. Payton just continued to frown.

"I'm very sorry," Lewis said. "I know how twins like to have their own identities and hate to get mixed up. Okay, Emma is Twin Number One. Got it."

Yes! I get to be Twin #1! was my first thought. But that was quickly followed up by the thought that we had accidentally twin-switched on set. This could be very confusing, particularly to my sister. We needed to just fix this now. Payton obviously felt the same way.

"Actually, I'm—" Payton and I both spoke up at the same time.

"Take two on my direction," the director said, cheerfully. "Look toward me a little bit when you frown, Emma."

"I'm—" I started to say.

"She's—" Payton started to say.

The assistant director jumped in front with the clapboard before we could say anything else.

"Teen Sheen, scene one, take four." She clapped the clipboard.

Action!

Voice-over Announcer: "These twins are so identical that it's usually hard to tell them apart. Until they didn't use identical shampoos."

Payton shook her greasy head.

"How did you get that shiny hair?" she asked me.

"I discovered the greatest new shampoo," I said, and flashed what I hoped was a dazzling smile.

"Cut!" the director called out. "Okay, I need you to say it with more oomph, Payton."

"Okay," Payton answered.

"No, I mean Payton," the director said. "You read your line fine, Emma. Payton can emphasize *greatest*."

He was totally mixing us up. Payton looked embarrassed. No way was I going to look and see what Ashlynn thought of that.

"Action!"

"How did you get that shiny hair?" Payton regrouped.

"I discovered the *greatest* new shampoo." I dazzle-smiled and held up the shampoo bottle.

Payton slithered her fingers through her grease and frowned.

"Cut!" the director said. "That was good. But, Payton, smile more."

Payton stopped frowning and smiled.

"No, not you, Emma," the director said. "Payton. Dazzle me, Payton."

Payton went back to frowning again. I widened my smile into a more dazzling smile. *Dazzle, Payton (Emma), dazzle!*

"Let's take it from 'Teen Sheen shampoo? That's what made your hair so supershiny?' Got it, Emma?"

I'm Payton, she's Emma. I'm Payton, she's Emma. I kept reminding myself. *Yeesh*, this was way more acting than

I'd anticipated. Acting my part, acting like my sister . . .

"Emma has a hair in her face!" the hairstylist called out. I felt around on my head for a hair and Payton did the same.

"No, Emma's hair." She pointed the brush at me.

"That's Payton," corrected the director, assistant director, and Ashlynn.

The hairstylist looked very confused. And that's when Ashlynn started cracking up. I looked at her and she shrugged innocently. And that's when I knew that Ashlynn was toying with us. I bet she knew all along that it was Payton, and she was just trying to throw Payton off her game. And boy, it worked. Ashlynn winked at me.

"Okay, twins . . . action!"

"Teen Sheen shampoo?" Payton asked me. "That's what made your hair so super twinny?"

"Cut!" the director said. "Shiny, not twinny!"

"I said 'twinny'? Oh my gosh, that was so stupid! Sorry," Payton said with a glance at Ashlynn, who was silently cracking up.

"Okay, let's reset. And . . . action!" the director said.

"Teen Sheen shampoo?" Payton asked me. "That's what made your hair so stupid shiny?"

"Cut!" the director said.

"Oh no! Sorry! Did I just say 'stupid shiny'?" Payton stammered. "*I'm* so stupid. But not stupid shiny."

Oh no, Payton was babbling. She was losing it. She kept glancing at a laughing Ashlynn.

"Ignore her," I hissed at Payton. Here she was, living her dream of being an actress on television, and she was letting Ashlynn get to her? I felt terrible for her. I thought of my own incident when I let Ben Becker, the Human Spell-Checker, shake my nerves of steel in the quarterfinal round of the fifth-grade spelling bee.

"Emma, try that line for me," the director said.

I could tell it wasn't going to be good. Payton was in the panic zone. And I couldn't even switch places and do it for her! Because we already were each other! And wait, that meant Emma—me—was the one who was screwing this up. Grrr. Ashlynn was ruining Payton's shoot and my reputation all at once. Double grrr.

"That's what made your hair so super liney?" Payton was saying. "That's what made your hair so snoopy shiny? I mean super hiney—"

Hiney? Oh my. Payton turned bright, bright and shiny red.

"Can we have a second?" I respectfully asked. "May I have a private moment with Payton?"

I realized my mistake a second too late when the crew joined Ashlynn in laughter.

"I mean, Emma!" I sputtered.

"They can't even tell themselves apart," I heard someone say.

I pulled Payton off to a quiet corner.

"I said *'hiney'*!" she wailed quietly.

"I know," I said. "Don't freak out. In through the nose, out through the mouth."

Payton tried to breathe more calmly.

"I know you can do this," I said. "This happened to me when Jazmine James gave me her special evil eye during mathletes and I said 'associative' instead of 'commutative.' I've regretted letting her get to me ever since. And you cannot let anything interfere with your dream. You want to be an actress, right?"

Payton nodded.

"Do you really want this to go well? Like as much as I wanted to win the Geobee?" I put my hands on her shoulders and looked her in the eyes.

"Yes," Payton said, sounding more confident. "I want this to go well as much as you wanted to win the Geobee. As much as you want to win mathletes and the spelling bee combined."

"Well." I frowned. "I'm not sure that's actually possible. They're held in different months. But I like your conviction. Okay, you're ready. Just focus on the words you need to say: That's what made your hair so supershiny."

"That's what made your hair so supershiny," Payton said.

"And Ashlynn is a super hiney," I said.

"And Ashlynn is . . ." Payton grinned. "Okay. Let's do it. Supershiny, supershiny."

We resumed our places. I sent her messages via twin telepathy. *You can do it, Payton (Emma)! Go, Twin #1!!*

"And, action!" the director shouted.

Voice-over Announcer: "These twins are
    so identical that it's usually hard to
    tell them apart. Until they didn't use
    identical shampoos."
Twin #1, aka Payton (Emma), shook
    her head of limp, greasy hair and
    frowned. Twin #2, aka me (Payton),
    smiled and shook her head of shiny,
    fabulous hair (slow motion).
Twin #1, aka Payton (Emma): Wow!

(gasped) How did you get that shiny hair?

Twin #2, aka Emma (Payton): I discovered the greatest new shampoo. (Held up shampoo bottle)

Twin #1, aka Payton (Emma), ran her fingers through her oily hair and frowned.

Twin #1, aka Payton (Emma): "Teen Sheen shampoo? That's what made your hair so supershiny?"

(Twin #2, a.k.a. Emma (Payton) nodded and tossed shampoo bottle to Twin #1, who caught it.)

"And, CUT!" the director said. "And that's a wrap! Excellent times two! Hurrah for the twins!"

Twin #1, aka Payton (Emma), and I grinned at each other. Yes! She did it! I did it! We did it! Woo-hoo!

I held out my hand and Payton joined me in our twin hand-clap-slap. We high-fived, low-fived, bumped fists, and yelled, "Twins rule!"

Thirteen

STUDIO SET

WE DID IT!

"Excellent times two! Hurrah for the twins!" the director said.

!!!!!!!!!!!!!!!!

When I accept my Academy Award, this is what I will say:

"Double thanks to my twin sister, Emma, who supported my acting career from the very beginning. Sure, my first role was as Greasy Hair Twin Number One in a shampoo commercial. But it was my launch to future glory in glamorous roles such as a princess in a TV series, a kick-hiney teen action hero in a movie, and now, my

Oscar-winning role as the girl who defeats a mean girl and empowers bullying victims everywhere. (The bully was based on some unknown named Ashlynn, who never got another role after her part in a shampoo commercial ended up on the cutting room floor.)"

Take that, Ashlynn! HA! HA! HA! Times two!

Emma

Fourteen

THE CRIB

I was glad Payton's confidence was boosted. But I was getting slightly tired of her babbling about the commercial shoot. We were back in our (shared) bedroom.

"And then, I just got in character," Payton said, for the three-hundred-squared time (Answer: nine hundred thousand). She was standing on her bed, reliving her glory. "I went into a zone, where I knew that no matter what Ashlynn did, I was going to say 'supershiny.'"

"Super," I murmured. Okay, back to Internet research. I tapped a few keys on the laptop and waited for it to load . . . loading . . . loading . . .

Payton was definitely in a better mood. Between the

shoot going so well and also discovering that the grease could be washed out of her hair in a matter of seconds (with Teen Scene special Power Clean shampoo), she was back to her shiny, clean self.

"My hair is kind of limp." Payton caught a glimpse of herself in the mirror. "Do you think I have time to curl it? Where's my curling iron?"

"Girls! Three-minute warning for dinner!" Dad knocked on our door.

"Already?" Payton said. "Hang on, let me throw my hair into a ponytail."

"Do I *have* to go?" I groaned. I had already wasted an entire day shooting the commercial and could use really use the additional time to work on my research for the upcoming science fair.

"You have to!" Payton said, nodding while pulling her hair back.

"Your producer was generous enough to set up the dinner." Dad nodded. "It would be rude not to go."

"That, too," Payton said. "But I was thinking you have to go because you can't miss the chance to go to one of the hottest, hippest, most now restaurants in LA. At least that's what it says on my restaurant app. We might see celebrities! It will seem like we *are* celebrities!"

"Haven't you figured out by now that I am not swayed by hottest, hippest, or 'most now'?" I told Payton. "And I prefer my celebrity to come from winning, for example, the Nobel Peace Prize and the National Spelling Bee (which also will result in a book and possibly a movie made about me)."

"But if you don't go," Payton said, "Dad will have to stay here with you, and that means I'll have to stay here too."

"It does sound enticing to stay in my man cave, watch the game, order pizza, and belch," Dad said thoughtfully.

Payton looked at me pleadingly. Oh, fine. So I shut the laptop, grabbed my phone with my new quiz app, and put on the denim dress that Payton was forcing me to wear.

I did perk up when I got a text message on my cell. *Brzzzzt!*

Maybe it was from Ox! But no, it was a video chat request. The profile picture was of a giant eyeball—a gecko's eyeball. Sigh. Mason.

"Hi, Emma!" He waved wildly at the camera. "How cool is it that you're in California! Look who misses you!"

Mascot the gecko's backside filled the screen. Sigh.

"Ha-ha-ha! Gecko butt from all the way across the country!" Mason yelled.

"Don't you need to be in bed?" I asked him. "It's late there."

"We are three hours ahead," Jason's voice came through. "Did you know the international date line was arbitrarily chosen?"

Brzzzzt!

"Ooh! A text message from Ox!" I blurted that out loud, unfortunately.

"Ooh, from Ox! Does it have lots of OOOs and XXXXs? Ox, ox, oxoxox? Smoochie smooch—"

They did not pay me enough for those twins. I hung up on Mason mid-smoochie.

Then I read Ox's text:

Hey, Hollywood! Did u know that the highest-grossing film ever is Avatar? An environmental activist movie! Maybe it's not so superficial out there after all! OX

"How do I look?" Payton came out of the bathroom wearing a cute white dress. She did a little *ta-da* move. "I'm so glad I got this new dress for Quinn's bat mitzvah already. Otherwise I probably would have brought Ashlynn's Summer Slave dresses. She'd never let me hear the end of that."

"You look great," I said, texting Ox. "I think your fuchsia scarf would look really good with it. I read that the fuchsia-and-white look is on trend on the West Coast."

Perhaps it wasn't as good as solving an extreme math problem, but the look on Payton's face when I solved her fashion dilemmas was somewhat rewarding. I texted Ox back while I waited for my twin.

Did u know the #2 movie is Titanic? A ship sinking into the ocean=not so uplifting or environmentally friendly. But on a happier Hollywood note, I'm on my way to a Hollywood "hot spot" for dinner. That's what Payton tells me, anyway.

Ox texted right back:

Factoid: In Japan, it is customary to remove your shoes when you enter a restaurant.

I responded:

Factoid: In Hollywood, it is customary to wear heels at least 4 inches high when entering a restaurant.

Ox replied:

Note to self: Next time I go to Hollywood, bring my 4 inch+ heels.

I texted back:

Ha-ha. Not guys. I have to go. I miss u.

I gulped at the last three words, and then I did it. I pressed send.

When Payton was ready, we headed downstairs to the main lobby. Dad had been told that someone from the crew would pick us up and take us to the restaurant. When we walked into the lobby I saw the two girls from the pool sitting on a couch and looking at an iPad.

"Hi!" Shira spotted us and waved.

"Let's go say hi to her," Payton said. I followed her over while Dad went to check out front for our ride.

"How did everything go today?" Shira asked. Then she glanced over toward her sister and added, "Don't give any incriminating details. My sister is spying as usual."

Her sister did not look up but she scowled.

"It was kind of crazy; nerve-racking but exciting!" Payton told her. "I loved it."

"It was fine," I said. "Payton is more of the actor in our family."

"I'm more of the actor in *my* family," Jessica said. Then she shot Shira a look.

"We have auditions tomorrow ourselves," Shira explained. "Jessica is unhappy that they called me in too. But I'm really excited."

"And delusional," Jessica muttered under her breath. But I caught that with my amazing lip-reading skills.

"I'm sure Shira has just as good a chance of getting a part as you," I said, so Jessica could hear.

"Yeah, right. I don't know why she's even bothering," Jessica said. "It's going to be yet another humiliating experience for you, Shira. Just like when the teachers ask you to read out loud in school and—"

"Stop it," Shira said, and I noticed she was turning red.

"I don't know what's going on, but it sounds like you're being out of line," I warned Jessica. Sheesh, fly across the continent just to find yet another mean girl. Were they everywhere?

"Actresses need to be able to read their lines," Jessica said. "It's no secret that Shira can barely read. It's going to make our whole family look like a joke if she auditions too."

Shira bit her lower lip.

"Shira, don't listen to her," Payton said. "I'm sure you'll do great. Your sister probably just feels threatened by you."

Jessica snorted.

"Embarrassed by her is more like it," Jessica said. "She makes me look bad in school and now she wants to act. I may need to get a stage name so nobody knows we're twins."

Whoa. Harsh.

"Jessica's right," Shira said. "I have stage fright, thanks to my stupid reading disorder. It *is* dumb for me to go in and audition. I mean, I can't even read the lines."

"That was so mean of you," Payton said, putting her hands on her hips and looked at Jessica. I was proud of Payton for standing up to Jessica, who was kind of intimidating—especially since Payton crumpled anytime Ashlynn looked her way.

I felt like I should back Payton up. She and Shira were both too nice to be crushed.

"Perhaps it's none of my business," I said, "but if you have a little time tomorrow morning I am quite an effective tutor. I'd be happy to go over some lines and tricks with you. My body clock is still on East Coast time, so I've been waking up very early."

"That's so nice of you," Shira said. "But it probably wouldn't help me."

"You should take her up on it," Payton said. "She helps me tons with memorizing and pronouncing words in my scripts. Plus she tutors these two hyper boys and their mother says she's worked miracles with them."

I smiled at Payton. That was nice of her. Plus it was true.

"Well, that would be nice," Shira said.

"She's probably just trying to find out more about your audition," Jessica said. "Don't divulge any information, because this role is *mine*."

I decided to ignore Jessica and plugged Shira's phone number into my cell. We made plans to meet in the main lobby to practice.

Our dad came into the lobby and called to us, "Girls, our car is here."

"Thanks, and see you in the morning." Shira smiled. Jessica ignored us.

We walked out to the car.

"Emma, that was so nice of you to offer to help her," Payton said.

"You sound so surprised," I said.

"Well, usually you're so focused on your own studying. And you're protective of your time," she said. "So this is really nice of you."

"I already have my lines for tomorrow memorized." I shrugged. "Plus it really bugged me that her sister kept putting her down. You'd think her twin would be supportive of her, not be her arch nemesis."

"Not everybody is so lucky to have a twin like you," Payton said, happily walking up to the car.

"You're awfully cheerful." Dad caught the tail end of what she was saying. "And I love to hear my twins complimenting each other."

"What's not to be cheerful about?" Payton said. "We're in Hollywood after shooting a commercial and now we're going to one of the 'hottest, hippest, most now' restaurants. It's perfect!"

The driver of the long black car opened the door and I spotted something inside.

"Not entirely perfect," I muttered to Payton. Ashlynn was sitting in the backseat. I watched as Payton's smile faltered as she spotted *her* arch nemesis.

"Hello." Dad slid behind Ashlynn and a lady I didn't recognize into the third row. "I'm Tom Mills, and these are my daughters, Emma and Payton."

"Hello," Ashlynn replied. "I'm Ashlynn, and this is my handler, Zoe."

I wondered briefly what a handler was, but decided whatever it was, I was happy Ashlynn had somebody there to handle her. I certainly didn't feel like doing it.

Payton shifted uncomfortably in the seat next to me as Ashlynn continued talking.

"I already know your daughters, sir," Ashlynn said in a sickly sweet voice that I remembered from summer camp when the counselor was around. "We went to summer camp and they assisted me with my off-Broadway debut."

"Now isn't that a wonderful coincidence!" Dad said, turning to look at us. "The girls didn't tell me they already knew somebody here in town."

"We didn't?" Payton said weakly. "Silly us."

"I know tons of people in town," Ashlynn said. "And I'm planning to know tons more because I'm flying home to New York City after this commercial for my great-aunt's dumb birthday party, but then I'm coming back for more auditions and pilot season—anything that could help me become a star."

"Ashlynn is certainly driven," the handler, Zoe, spoke up. "Is this your girls' first shoot?"

"Yes," Dad said. "I think it's a nice experience for them as well as a little vacation."

"Are you enjoying yourselves?" Zoe asked.

"It's pretty fun," I said. "But I can see how it would get a little monotonous being on the set sometimes. Lots of waiting, not many lines to memorize."

"Monotonous?" Payton turned to me. "It's the opposite of monotonous! It's so interesting, not only when you're acting, but also to see everything that's going on around you. I love watching how the director sets up the shoot, how the camerapeople plan their angles, and then that magic moment when they say 'action'!"

Payton clapped her hands together, smiling.

"It seems you've caught the bug," Zoe said. "I, too, feel that the action behind the scenes and the energy of the industry is exciting."

"As long as I'm captured on camera, the rest is whatever." Ashlynn waved it off with attitude.

"I think the rest is just as exciting," Payton said. "And definitely important! When you think of all of the pieces that have to come together —the writers writing the lines, the people finding the right location, and people like you, Zoe, who work with the actors behind the scenes. All to capture something on camera for the audience to hopefully connect with."

I gaped at my sister. She sounded like she really knew what she was talking about. I've never seen her so into anything. She looked like me last week when I still thought I was competing in the Geobee and was color-coding my flash cards.

Plus, she totally shut Ashlynn down, and not even on purpose. Payton and Zoe were in an intense discussion about the "industry." Ashlynn and I just sat there quietly the rest of the ride. But while Ashlynn was annoyed, I was smiling.

Go, Payton! Watching my sister shine was almost worth missing the Geobee.

Fifteen

HOLLYWOOD HOT SPOT

Ashlynn perked up when she saw the restaurant. "You know who goes to this restaurant?" she said, and then started naming celebrities. Some I knew and some I didn't.

"I hope we see some celebrities tonight!" I said.

"I know!" Ashlynn smiled at me and I smiled back. We had a moment of solidarity—well, less than a moment. Ashlynn dropped her smile and then assumed her usual snooty look. I looked away.

"Of course, tons of celebrities are in New York City, where I live, so it's not that big a deal," Ashlynn said. "Plus, soon I'll be on Broadway, and then *I'll* be a celebrity."

My father gave me a quizzical look. *Yep, get the*

picture, Dad? But even Ashlynn couldn't dampen my excitement as we walked into the restaurant.

"How cool is this, Emma? We're going to a Hollywood hot spot," I said as we walked in together. "And how cool is Zoe? She totally knows so much about the entertainment business."

"Try to get a seat next to her," Emma advised me. "It's never too early to explore career possibilities. Remember when the mathematician came in on third grade parents' career day and I picked her brain?"

How could I forget? The teacher had to ask Emma twice to stop monopolizing the Q&A time and then practically had to pry Emma off the woman's leg.

"And let's both try to avoid sitting next to Ashlynn," Emma said. Agreed!

However, that turned out to be impossible because it ended up there was only one person joining us: a man named George who worked at the Teen Scene shampoo company. We sat at a long table, with me, Emma, and Ashlynn on one side and Dad, George, and Zoe on the other.

"Thank you for having us," Emma said to George.

"We're having so much fun!" I told him. "This is an amazing opportunity!"

"We wanted to treat you for your hard work today.

And we thought you three girls might enjoy spending some time together," George said. "Lewis sends his regards, but he is editing tonight."

We ordered our food. I got penne with chicken and alfredo sauce, Emma got linguini with clam sauce, and Ashlynn ordered a shrimp Caesar salad. The server brought out bread with olive oil and we started nibbling.

It turned out George was a vice president of marketing and sales, which is what our dad is, so they got in a big bonding session over the state of the industry blah blah finances.

"So, Zoe, what exactly does a handler do?" I asked Zoe. She gave us a full-out description. It was fascinating! Celebrities! Events! Backstage scoop!

"So, Payton, are you going back to camp this year?" Ashlynn suddenly startled me by interrupting us.

"Um," I said, turning away from Zoe. "I don't know yet."

"I am. But I'm also going to this musical theater camp where famous producers come and I might get discovered and—" Ashlynn went on and on. Zoe turned to Dad and George and started talking.

"So, Ashlynn," Emma finally interrupted Ashlynn's monologue. "I noticed you didn't film anything today.

Are you really in the commercial or were you just there to cheer us on?"

"Yes, I'm in the commercial," she snapped.

Hee.

"I thought maybe they cut your part," Emma said, looking falsely concerned.

"I have a part," she said. "They just didn't get to mine today."

"Sure, mm-hmm," Emma said. Hee!

"I'm ignoring you," Ashlynn said, pulling out her phone and beginning to text. I enjoyed how her face got all red. Heh.

I looked around the restaurant, which was pretty cool. It wasn't a fancy place and it had a laid-back feel to it. Very California. People were dressed in summer dresses or shorts and flip-flops. Some people were very glamorous and looked like celebrities.

Hmm. I looked closer at one of the women. It looked like . . .

"Emma, look!" I whispered. "It's the actress who plays the doctor on that show I like."

Emma craned her neck to get a better look.

"What are you two making a scene about?" Ashlynn rolled her eyes.

"Look who's sitting at that table," Emma said. "Payton spotted her."

"Well don't go asking for her autograph or anything," Ashton said. "That's so touristy. Celebrities are just regular people. Right, Zoe?"

"They are certainly regular people but that doesn't mean we can't get excited when we spot them," Zoe said. "Even though I work with celebrities, I still get starstruck around some of my favorites."

"I don't think I would ever get used to being around celebrities." I sighed. "Zoe, you have the coolest job."

"Thanks." Zoe looked pleased. "I do work hard, but it's rewarding and fun. Payton, why don't you go take a closer look at the celebrity you spotted."

"Really?" I glanced at Ashlynn to see her reaction.

"It's your first celebrity sighting." Zoe smiled. "Just casually walk past her. I know you won't be obtrusive."

"Excuse me, but I have to go to the *ladies' room*." I hopped up and walked back to the ladies' room. I tried to be inconspicuous, like la la la, just going to the bathroom. Not slowing down at all when walking by a TV star's table and possibly peeking just a little bit at her. La la la!

The actress was talking to a friend but she looked up briefly when I walked by. I was busted! But she smiled at me. So I was busted but the actress didn't mind! She smiled at me!

Oh my gosh oh my gosh oh my gosh!

I splashed a little cold water on my face from the bathroom sink to cool myself down. But it was understandable that I was all red and flushed. I just had my first celebrity sighting! I was about one foot—no, maybe even ten inches—from a real, live celebrity! A real, live celebrity smiled at me!

And I had smiled back! I smiled into the mirror just like I had smiled back at the actress. Wait, my smile looked weird. Is that how I smiled at her? I looked like a weirdo. Wait. Is that how I smiled while filming my commercial today? I thought about it and realized that I'd only frowned about having oily hair in the commercial today. But tomorrow my role included smiling. I had better practice my smile.

I smiled. No, too dorky. I smiled again. Too wide and toothy. The next one looked too fake. Then not happy enough. Then—

The door opened and my smile completely disappeared.

"Staring at the mirror won't make you suddenly better-looking," Ashlynn said, shutting the door behind her.

"I was just leaving," I said. I tried to go out the door but Ashlynn blocked it.

"I'm sure you're anxious to get back to Zoe," Ashlynn said. "My, and I emphasize *my*, handler."

"I know she's your handler," I said, confused.

"*I know* you're trying to steal her from me," Ashlynn accused.

"What?" I sputtered.

"You're so totally obvious with all of your sucking up to her. You're always jealous of me and want to be like me. You wear my clothes, you try to steal the limelight at my Broadway show—"

"Off-off-Broadway," I blurted out. Mistake. She glared at me harder.

"And now you're trying to steal my handler," Ashlynn said. "Oh, and by the way, nice attempt at stealing your sister's identity yesterday. I almost fell for it except that I could tell that you get all starstruck around me and she doesn't."

Not starstruck, but definitely dumbstruck. I opened my mouth and could not think of a comeback. Because she was right. I had pretended to be Emma because she threw me. But I certainly wasn't trying to steal her handler.

"Emma isn't starstruck around me because she's oblivious," Ashlynn said. "She thinks she's so smart but she's just a dumb nerd."

What? Did she just call my sister dumb?

"A nerd is not an insult," I said. "And obviously Emma is the opposite of dumb. I'm heading back to the table. If you want to talk to Zoe instead of texting rudely under the table, go right ahead. Otherwise I'm going to keep talking to her because I think she's fascinating."

There! I did it! I spoke my mind to Ashlynn. I reached across her and pushed the bathroom door open. Then I held my head up high as I walked out onto the patio and past the actress's table.

And then I heard somebody whisper behind me, "Who do you think you are, talking to *me* like that?"

It was Ashlynn. And I could not believe what Ashlynn did next. She stepped on the back of the heel of my shoe. I think she only meant to make me stumble a little bit, but even Ashlynn didn't realize how completely uncoordinated I could be. I stumbled, all right, then I tripped and bumped—right into the actress's table.

"Ooph!" I made a loud noise. I could see Emma racing over to help me. But it was too late.

I tried to push away so I wouldn't face-plant on the

actress's table, but it tipped and I lost control. I could hear Ashlynn laughing as I started falling backward. . . .

I was falling! I was falling and dying of embarrassment at the same time! I was going to fall on the table of the people behind me! I waved my hands wildly in the air, trying to catch myself when suddenly—

Someone else caught me! I heard everyone gasp. I felt arms grab me before I hit the floor, and I was tipping backward, caught in the arms of . . . of . . .

A flashing light suddenly blinded me and I blinked. When my vision unblurred I saw the face of the person who had caught me:

Singing star and YouTube sensation Dustin Weaver.

?????

!!!!!

Obviously I had hit my head and was delirious because it looked like Dustin Weaver was holding me in his arms. Well, if I was going to be delirious, this was certainly a nice hallucination. I could gaze at his piercing blue eyes and his dark brown hair that curled over his ears, and hear his gruff-yet-gentle voice.

"Are you okay?" he asked me. Ahh. Dustin Weaver Hallucination was concerned about my well-being. Ahh. He set me gently back on my feet.

Also, in my hallucination I could enjoy the facial expressions of an envious Ashlynn and a shocked Emma. My vision was so vivid and realistic.

There was a sudden flurry of activity, and a large man jumped between me and Dustin.

"Do I need to call security or will you leave of your own accord?" the large man growled at me.

This hallucination was taking a very strange and unpleasant turn.

"It was an accident!" Emma jumped between me and the man who had jumped between me and daydream Dustin Weaver. "My sister is a klutz and just tripped."

Wait a minute. This *was* a hallucination, wasn't it?

"You didn't fling yourself at Dustin?" the large man asked me suspiciously.

"Relax, Hank, she really tripped," Dustin said. "I saw her bump into that table and then fall backward, so I caught her."

I looked around wildly.

"Am I dreaming? Did I hit my head and now I'm fantasizing that Dustin Weaver caught me?" I asked.

Everyone started laughing.

"See, Hank, I told you it was an accident," Dustin said.

"Maybe not totally an accident," Emma muttered.

She put her arm around me and squinted narrowly at Ashlynn. Emma must have seen Ashlynn trip me! But Ashlynn wasn't paying attention to Emma.

She was standing there with her mouth open.

"You're Dustin Weaver," she finally said. "I love you."

Dustin suddenly looked uncomfortable and the bodyguard jumped in front of him.

"Okay, show's over people," the bodyguard announced. "Let Dustin eat his meal in peace."

"But wait! Dustin! I love you!" Ashlynn called out. "Will you marry me?"

"Sorry about her," Emma said to Dustin. "She drives us crazy too."

"Dustin! I'll give you my cell number!" Ashlynn looked wild-eyed.

"Hey, I'm glad you're okay," he called to me and then slid behind his bodyguard.

"Thanks for catching me," I squeaked and then walked quickly with Emma back toward our table. I collapsed onto my chair and gasped.

"I can't believe that just happened. Dustin Weaver! He held me in his arms!" I said.

AHHHHHHH! DUSTIN WEAVER HELD ME IN HIS ARMS!

Oh man, wait until I told everyone back home. Tess was a superfan of his and even blogged about him on her DustinWeaverMath site, where she listed numerical facts like how many Flitter followers he has (one million as of last weekend), and how many number-one singles (five), and how many tattoos (zero). Emma liked to do Tess's Word Puzzle of the Week, but I went on the site for the photos. Sydney and Cashmere were going to freak out.

AHHH! I was freaking out! Emma just sat calmly next to me.

Ashlynn looked like she was still in shock.

"Well, you ladies were gone a long time," my father said.

"Oh you know how girls are, always chitchatting in the bathroom together," Zoe said.

"We saw Dustin Weaver!" I said. "He is a *huge* star," I added. (A gorgeous, gorgeous huge star!)

Emma explained what had happened, "And thanks to Ashlynn, Payton got to . . . hug him," she finished, shooting Ashlynn a look.

Ashlynn was still in shock.

Hee. And hee.

"How nice of Ashlynn to help you meet one of your favorite celebrities," Dad said. I would've corrected him but, hey. After all, if she hadn't tripped me, I wouldn't have fallen, so I guess he was technically correct. But who cared how it happened. What was important was that I talked to . . . was cradled in the arms of . . .

Dustin Weaver!

AHHHHHHHHHHHHHH!!!!!!!

I was still happily reeling while George paid the bill, and then it was time to go. We walked out of the restaurant and into a pack of paparazzi that had gathered outside the door.

"They must be waiting for Dustin," Zoe said. "I don't envy his handler. That must be a challenging job to try to protect him from the press and his fans."

Ashlynn whimpered a bit.

As we got back into the car, Ashlynn regained her composure. She opened her mirror and reapplied some lip gloss.

"Anyway," she suddenly said. "It's not like anyone will really believe you talked to Dustin Weaver."

"What are you talking about?" Emma said. "I was there, Payton was there, and you were there."

"I'll deny it. Then who will believe the two of you?" Ashlynn scoffed. "*Suuuuure* you met Dustin Weaver."

I sat between Emma and Dad in the second row of

145

seats and alternated between being furious at Ashlynn and being ecstatic that I met Dustin, and being bummed that even if I did tell people, they might not believe me. I wished I had a picture of us. One that left out the embarassing tripping and falling. Just us a simple picture of me talking to Dustin Weaver. It would have been nice to have some photographic evidence of my Hollywood Celebrity Encounter.

Emma

Sixteen

IN LIMO LEAVING HOLLYWOOD HOT SPOT

I stared at my cell phone. A picture had loaded and there, somehow, was a picture of Payton. And Dustin Weaver. Payton was leaning over backward and Dustin was catching her in his arms.

It made no sense. I didn't take the photo. It had been sent to me. By Tess! How did Tess have a picture of something that happened a few minutes ago here in California?

"Emma"—my dad cleared his throat—"Zoe just asked you a question." The subtext being, *Don't be rude texting in company; please rejoin the conversation.*

I shoved my phone in my bag without shutting it

off. I hoped the photo wouldn't delete itself, or that my phone wouldn't self-destruct, or . . .

"Emma?" Zoe leaned forward in her seat. "I was curious about how *you* enjoyed the filming today. Your sister certainly enjoyed it."

The limo we were all riding in took a sharp turn. I fell a little sideways onto Payton—and, oh no, my bag. I sneaked a peek into it. Payton and Dustin were still there, in two-dimensional pixilated form.

"Yes," I said. "Today was fine. No complaints."

"Fine?" Payton said. "It was awesome. I loved everything about it. Well, maybe not the greasy hair, but everything else."

Ashlynn snorted.

The car pulled into the apartment complex parking lot.

"So you guys are staying here too?" Payton asked Zoe and Ashlynn as we pulled up into the complex. "You don't live in LA, Zoe?"

"I do, but I'm staying with Ashlynn while she's here," Zoe said.

"My very own handler," Ashlynn said smugly.

"How nice that you two can travel together," Dad said cheerfully.

 148

"Oh, I just met Zoe yesterday." Ashlynn shrugged. "My mother hired her for this shoot."

My sister and I looked at each other. I couldn't imagine traveling across the country without anyone in my family and staying with somebody I just met.

I felt suddenly sorry for Ashlynn.

"Zoe, you need to staple all my new headshots to my bio while you're at it in case I meet any bigwigs tomorrow," Ashlynn commanded. "The talent—that's me—is going to soak in the hot tub and relax."

And then I didn't feel sorry for Ashlynn. We all got out of the car and said good-bye.

"I think I'm going to take a walk," Dad said.

"You're going to the little store for snacks, aren't you?" Payton teased.

"It's not a man cave without snacks," Dad admitted. After taking our orders, he gave us the keys to our apartment and told us he'd meet us back there. Payton ordered cheese puffs; I ordered twisty pretzels.

"What a nightmare Ashlynn is. Can you imagine working for her? Poor Zoe," Payton shook her head.

"You pretty much worked for her as Summer Slave," I reminded her as I put the key into the door of the apartment. "I hope Zoe is getting paid better than you did."

"You're right! Poor me! It was so funny when Ashlynn turned into a Dustin Weaver Stalker." Payton giggled. "I love you! Marry me!"

"And that's the perfect segue into what I'm going to show you," I said as we walked inside. "I have a surprise for you. Brace yourself."

I gave Payton the phone and she looked at it, puzzled.

"You have thirteen new text messages?" she said. "Okay."

"Wait, what?" I looked. She was right. "I thought it was pulled up to a picture. When did all these messages come in?"

I took back my phone. I quickly read the first text from Tess, the one that had been sent with the photo.

I saw this on a Dustin Weaver fan site! OMG! Tell me more!

"Oh, my phone is still off from dinner," Payton remembered. She pulled out her own phone and turned it on while I scrolled through my messages to see if any were important (Ox), but they were from was Tess, Quinn, and . . . Sydney? Cashmere? Oh, the photo must be making the rounds.

"I have fourteen new messages," Payton was saying. "People must really miss us at home. Look, Tess,

Quinn, wait—Sydney? Nick—yay! Quinn again, Sydney, Cashmere, Cashmere again . . . ?"

"I think I may know why they're all texting," I told her. Then I pulled up the picture that Tess had sent and handed the phone to my twin.

She looked at it and her eyes got wide.

"Is that me?" Payton squinted at the picture. "Is that a picture of me falling?"

"Yes." I nodded. "And Dustin Weaver catching you. A fan must've taken the picture and put it up on Dustin Weaver's fan site. So now you have your documentation that you met Dustin Weaver. Just like you wanted!"

"That is so cool!" Payton said. She jumped up and down around the kitchen area. Then she stopped and grinned. "Oh, is that why everyone is texting us?"

"Tess found it first," I said. "She's the one who sent it to me, really fast."

"Tess is an überfan," Payton told me.

"Huh," I said. "I wouldn't have guessed that. I mean, she's a former mathlete."

"What, mathletes can't like pop stars?" Payton looked at me funny. "Like they can't like *fashion*?"

Oops. Like me.

"Sorry." I blushed. "Old stereotypes die hard."

"Anyway, I know Cashmere's a superüberfan," Payton went on. "She must have told Sydney. Eeeee! This is so awesome! People at home are seeing me with Dustin Weaver! I need to call Tess!"

She tossed me back my phone and picked up hers.

Just then we heard the door buzz. We let Dad in.

"I've got pretzels and nachos and those puffs that turn your fingers orange that your Mom doesn't let us eat in the house," he said, holding up a brown paper bag like it was a prize.

"Oh that's great, Dad," I said. "Woo-hoo."

"So, let's all sit down and pig out." Dad beamed. He started laying out the bags of food along with three bottles of water.

I looked at my sister. *Now what?*

"Um, Dad," Payton said, "first Emma and I need to go in our room and—er—rehearse our lines."

"Girls." Our father looked at us both. "I know you're all jazzed up about Hollywood and all, but I think we should settle down and have some quality time as a family."

Payton and I reluctantly put our phones down and sat on the couch. The three of us then spent quality time together watching a singing competition.

"Now that's one competition Emma wouldn't win," Dad joked.

"*Ha-ha!* Good one," I said. Payton and I gave him a kiss goodnight and then—

"Finally!" Payton gasped, shutting the door behind me. "I have to see what's going on!"

"You're getting cheese powder all over your phone," I pointed out as Payton pulled hers out of her bag.

"Okay, here's the plan," my twin said. "I'll text Tess while you see what it looks like on the fan site."

"Um," I said. "Remember the time difference. They are three hours ahead of us, so it's already the middle of the night at home."

"Crumbcakes!" Payton frowned. "I can't believe I'll have to wait till tomorrow morning to tell everybody all about it. Do I have to tell them exactly how it happened? The embarrassing part about tripping and falling, too? That's so embarrassing. Let's not tell them. Just say . . . hmm . . ."

I had a sudden thought. I wondered if the fan who had posted on the website had also posted a caption. Like, "Random girl almost trips and face-plants! Is saved by Dustin Weaver!" I hadn't looked for any caption. I didn't want Payton to worry needlessly, so I casually clicked on the picture and waited until the link took me to the Internet. The picture loaded . . . loaded . . .

Yes, there was a caption below:

Who is Dustin Weaver's New Mystery Girlfriend?

Okay, wait—what? I reread the headline.

Who is Dustin Weaver's New Mystery Girlfriend?

And then below: *Click the link for the exclusive scoop!*

Exclusive scoop? I clicked the link and read on.

Dustin Weaver took his new mystery girl on a dinner date and we captured them in a romantic embrace! Don't worry, DustinFans, we'll track down who his new mystery love really is!

Date? Mystery love? Romantic embrace???!! My mind struggled to logically make sense of this.

"Emma?" Payton asked. "Are you okay? You look pale and dizzy. Is it jet lag?"

"No." I held up the phone. "There's something you need to see. But first, sit down."

"Okay," Payton said cheerfully. She sat down on her bed and took my phone again. I watched as the color drained from my sister's face.

"They said I'm Dustin's new girlfriend? Me? They said we were having a ROMANTIC EMBRACE?" Payton gasped.

"Well, I guess from the angle they captured you, it does rather look like you're in his arms and he is gazing at you." I nodded. "I could see that interpretation."

"Besides the fact that none of that is true." Payton gasped again. "I'm way too young for Dustin Weaver. He's fifteen. I'm in seventh grade! What are they thinking?"

"I don't think you can really tell how old you are in this picture." I examined it closely. "Since you are in mid-fall, you are in motion, and a little blurry. Possibly blurry enough that nobody would be able to identify you, except obviously our friends, like Tess. That's good."

"Oh, you're right," Payton said. "All of his fans would come after me. We better make sure that Sydney and everyone doesn't post my identity on the site."

"On the positive side, it looks like this site doesn't accept comments," I said after I checked. "So people aren't putting anything crazy on there. Although of course this can get reposted on other sites and then . . ."

"We'd better tell Dad," Payton said. We went into the living room, but Dad wasn't there. We knocked on the door to the man cave but there was no answer. I pecked inside and saw my father sprawled out on the bed, sleeping, the remains of a bag of nacho chips next to him.

"Looks like jet lag got him," I said. I closed the door and grabbed a couple of pretzels. I sat down on the couch and ate.

"Should we call Mom?" Payton asked.

"It's really late," I said. "I don't think it's worth waking her up. What can she do, anyway? We'll have to wait for morning to talk to Dad and straighten everything out with our friends back home."

"You don't think any of our friends from home believe that 'romance' story, do you? I mean, it's flattering and all . . ." Payton's voice trailed off. "Oh no, I just had a terrible thought. What if somebody shows it to Nick? What if Nick thinks I was on a romantic date with someone else?"

"I highly doubt Nick would believe that. Nobody could seriously believe this," I said, popping a pretzel into my mouth. I wondered what they did think, though.

I opened a text message from Quinn:

DUSTIN WEAVER'S DATE? WHAT IS THIS?

Uh-oh. Maybe someone *would* believe this. I opened up a text message from Cashmere and read it.

I just saw 1 of u guys on a DUSTIN WEAVER fan site!!! Which 1 of u is Dustin's new love: U or PAYTON?!?! OMG!!!!

Wait a minute, me or Payton? *Me* or Payton? Why didn't this occur to me before? The article didn't have Payton's name in it! Of course people might think it's ME! ME on a mystery date with Dustin Weaver?

"Well, Nick's text is normal," Payton said. "He just says he hopes I'm having fun in Hollywood. Wait, then he says he has to go because Sydney is calling him."

Payton looked up at me.

"Oh no, she was probably calling him to see if he saw the picture on the website." Payton looked at her phone. "That was three hours ago and he hasn't texted me back. And he probably thinks I'm ignoring his text. And what if he thinks I'm not answering his text because I'm ON A DATE WITH DUSTIN WEAVER?!"

While Payton was freaking out, I was slowly having a sinking feeling myself. Ox hadn't texted me at all in a few hours. Normally I wouldn't think twice about that. But he hadn't responded to my last text.

"Oh, this text from Tess makes me feel much better." Payton exhaled a sigh of relief. "She thinks that the picture is you, Emma, because of the ponytail."

We both looked at each other and realized that Payton was wearing a ponytail. And of course usually the twin who wore a ponytail was . . .

Me.

"Oh. OH. Sorry! They think it's YOU, Emma! Sorry!" Payton cringed. "Oh no, what if Nick thinks it's me and Ox thinks it's you . . ."

Her voice trailed off.

"Uh-oh," Payton said. "Did you happen to get any texts from Ox?"

I slowly shook my head. *Uh-oh* was right.

Seventeen

THE CRIB

"Good morning, girls!" Dad sang out cheerfully. "Rise and shine! It's a beautiful day in LA."

I looked up to see the sun shining through the window.

"What time is it?" Emma yawned.

"Eight thirty," Dad said.

"What?!" Emma said. "Didn't my alarm go off?"

"Man, that alarm is loud," Dad said. "I came in here and you both were sleeping through the noise. I turned it off for you. It was only four o'clock."

"I know," Emma told him. "I set my alarm for four so I could text with Ox before school started back home. They're three hours behind us, remember?"

"Sorry," Dad groaned. "I thought you did that as a mistake, because of the time difference. I thought it would be better to set it for eight thirty so you'd get more sleep."

"Now I missed the opportunity to text Ox," Emma wailed. "He's in school!"

"Emma, you are too young to be so attached to texting a young man. You can text him later," my father scolded.

"It's not that! I have to explain to him—and wait, we have to explain to you, too—what we found out last night," Emma protested.

"Wait a minute." I was fully awake now. "We have our shoot this morning!"

"Yes," Dad said. "Luckily we don't have to leave for the studio until nine, so you have plenty of time to get ready. And you both got a good night's sleep."

"Dad!" It was my turn to wail. "We can't get ready in just a half hour! Even Emma can't get ready in a half hour."

"I'm sorry. I knew you didn't have to wash your hair because it's supposed to be greasy or your hairstylist people would do it." Dad looked upset. "And you didn't have to put on your makeup because you have makeup people. Plus, a half hour seemed like a long time to me."

"It's okay, Dad." I jumped out of bed. "However, since I have only a half hour to take a shower and get dressed . . . get out of my way! I call the master bathroom!"

"Actually, you have twenty-seven minutes," Emma said, her efficient self taking over.

I took my cue from her—no more thinking about boys. For now. I didn't have time to worry about the whole Dustin Weaver thing—I had to focus. I repeated my lines for the commercial over and over again in the shower. Teen Sheen! Shiny *and* shiny! Double the shiny!

Emma was ready way before me, of course. While I was racing around the room looking for a sandal, her cell phone buzzed with a text message.

"Maybe it's Ox! Or at least somebody from home who can talk to Ox," Emma said and looked at her phone. "Oh, it's Shira. Oh no, I was supposed to help Shira! Well, I still have fourteen minutes. I can do a power-tutoring session."

Emma made arrangements to meet with Shira down in the lobby.

"That's really nice of you to help her," I said.

"Oh, no problem." Emma waved her hand dismissively.

When I was ready, Dad and I went down to the lobby and found Emma, Shira, and their mom on a couch.

"Guess what?" Emma said. "Shira is auditioning at the same studio we are, so I offered to share a ride and help her along the way."

"Thank you so much for offering to help Shira," her mother said. "This means a lot. But is this a problem?"

Dad reassured her it wasn't at all.

Then I heard a voice behind me and I jumped.

"It's not like you're going to be able do anything." Jessica had come up behind us. She spoke softly, so our parents couldn't hear. "Even our teachers practically gave up on her."

I opened my mouth to say something back, but Emma gave me a look to keep my mouth closed. Then she winked at me, so I knew she had a plan. As we all climbed into the car Emma fixed it so she was in the way back with Shira. Jessica climbed in, then her mother, then me and Dad in the middle seat.

"Okay," I heard Emma say. "Let me just give you a quick test to see how you learn best."

"A test?" Shira sounded panicked.

"No, no, this is a fun test." Emma laughed. "Yes, there is such a thing. It'll take thirty seconds. . . ."

Wow, I thought. *Emma sounds so relaxed and in control.* Emma really had a knack for tutoring. Jessica put on headphones right away. Good, then she wouldn't benefit from Emma's tips. She didn't deserve them.

Dad and the twins' mother were talking and it turned out that she used to be a doctor at a hospital that used Dad's supplies. They knew the same people blah blah.

"What a small world!" she was saying. "You know Joe, too? How about Mary? Blah blah blah—"

Then I heard Dad's cell go off.

"Excuse me, girls?" Dad said. "I just got the schedule texted to me. Apparently Ashlynn is filming first. Twin Number One, you need to arrive earlier, and Twin Number Two doesn't have a call time until noon."

"I'm Twin Number Two," Emma said, "so that works out great. Hey, Shira, since we're on the same studio lot and my call time isn't until noon, why don't I go with you to your audition and prep you until you're called?"

"Emma, that's so nice, but you have your own commercial to film," Shira protested.

"I'll just be standing around doing nothing," Emma

said. "I already have my lines memorized, so I'm ready to go. Payton, do you need me for anything?"

"Nope," I said. "I probably have to go in earlier so they can get my hair all oiled up. Then I'm shooting some scenes just by myself without Emma, so it's fine."

Their mom thought that was really nice, and Dad said that was fine with him as long as Emma had her cell phone and stayed with Shira's mother.

"Text me when you're ready and I'll come over and get you or Shira and Jessica's mom can bring you to us," Dad said.

I knew that Emma wasn't going to let her phone leave her side since she was waiting to hear from Ox. When the car pulled into the studio lot, we all climbed out.

Jessica took her headphones off when she saw Emma leaving with them.

"Why is she coming with us?" I heard her say. I smiled as I walked in the other direction to our new studio, Studio 3, with Dad.

Studio 3! Where I was filming my commercial: Teen Sheen scenes two, three, and four!

It was kind of crazy to walk onto the set and feel so comfortable. I felt like a pro! The first place I was scheduled to go was to see the hairstylist, Jean-Marie. Not my favorite time, greasy time, but hey! I was a professional at this now. Grease me up, Jean-Marie! I walked over confidently and . . .

Bluh. Ashlynn was in the chair getting her hair done.

"I just don't think it looks as good as it could," I heard Ashlynn complain. "I think you need to try again."

Then Ashlynn pulled out the barrette that was in her hair and shook her hair out. I could see the hairstylist's fist clenching and a look of frustration on her face. She brushed Ashlynn's hair and clipped the barrette back in.

"I'm not sure that it's right yet—" Ashlynn was interrupted as Zoe ran up to her and told her she was needed on the set.

"Oh, hi, Payton." She smiled at me. "Ready for more shooting?"

"Definitely!" I said.

"I'm ready too," Ashlynn muttered—and shot Jean-Marie a dirty look. Yikes.

"Hi, Ashlynn," I said.

"Oh, is it time for your grease? On second look, your hair looks greasy enough."

I tried not to let her bother me as I climbed up into the chair.

"Did she just say what I think she said?" Jean-Marie

asked me. "Hmm. I thought I saw her giving you and your twin some attitude on the set yesterday."

"I'm trying not to let her bother me," I said. "But it's a challenge."

"That girl has been a real diva," Jean-Marie said. "I wish that she had your role in the commercial so that I could dump a bucket of grease on her head."

I grinned.

"Where is that twin sister of yours, anyway?" Jean-Marie asked. "She was a real help to me yesterday."

"Really?" I didn't know that. I tipped my hair back into the sink and Jean-Marie rinsed my hair.

"I'm studying for a special license and she saw my exam booklet," Jean-Marie said. "Emma gave me some tips on how to remember some of the material while I was doing her hair. She's a real whiz, isn't she?"

"Yes, she is," I said. "She's even helping another girl with her audition right now. I'd help you out if I could, but my brain doesn't work like hers does."

"Well I hear you have acting talent, so don't sell yourself short. You two are nice girls," the hairstylist said. "You don't always get that in this industry."

I relaxed while she put on the goopy grease. It felt slick and oozing against my head.

"You are right about the grease coming off my hair last night," I told her. "I went out to dinner last night and you could barely tell."

While she was slicking my hair strands I thought about the previous night. I still couldn't believe that I'd had close personal contact with Dustin Weaver. *Squee!* And that someone had posted on a blog that I (Payton) was on a mystery date with him. *Ack!*

It was a rollercoaster of emotions.

"It looks like I have to give you grease on your hair for the morning shot," Jean-Marie explained. "But then you finally get to have clean, shiny hair for this afternoon's shot," she said.

Yay! Clean, shiny hair! And then she told me I was good to go. Next I went to wardrobe and makeup, where I had my makeup done and go dressed. (In the same outfit as yesterday. Hopefully washed.)

I noticed Dad over at the craft services table, eating some snacks. Between his man cave and endless snacks, I was glad he was having a good trip.

So, there I was. Ready to go. With nothing to do. I didn't want to eat anything in case I smudged my lipstick. I could see Ashlynn filming a scene. I was tempted to go watch her, but I had the greasy hair.

Well, she'd seen my greasy hair look already. And I wanted to see what she was doing. I hated to admit it, but I knew from camp and the off-Broadway show that she was a really good actor. Maybe I could learn something from her.

I stood off to the side as Ashlynn flipped her hair around and said "Teen Sheen Shampoo! For supershiny hair!"

"And, cut!" the director said. "That's a wrap for you on this scene. You have one more later today."

"Watch and learn, Greasy," Ashlynn said as she passed me. "Watch and learn. You and your sister may have gotten this gig because you're freaks of nature, but I got it for sheer talent. And for my looks."

Erg, she bothered me so much. And then I worried that it was true. Obviously we were here for our twinness, but I hoped I could prove that I had talent.

Wait a minute. Speaking of twins . . . Where was Emma? I went over to my father and asked if he'd seen Emma.

"I have not," he said.

He called Shira's mom. While he was talking, I texted Emma.

Are you here yet? It's time!

"Shira is still in her audition," Dad reported back. "So her mom can't leave. I'll go pick up Emma and race back here in a jiffy."

"Hurry," I begged.

"Twin Number One, you're up." The assistant director called. I put my phone down on a chair near Jean-Marie. The AD went over my lines and what I was supposed to do and I went to my mark in front of the camera. It was weird to be out there without Emma.

"Teen Sheen Shampoo, scene two, take one!" The AD clapped the clapboard.

"I've *got* to try Teen Sheen Shampoo." I frowned and ran my fingers through my hair. That was the first take. The director decided I shouldn't run my fingers through my hair, but I should shake my head so my greasy hair would flop all over unattractively.

Take two. I shook my head and tried to be unattractive. They didn't like the camera angle. Take three. I did it again.

"Something about this isn't working for me," the director said. "Don't worry, it's not you, Twin Number One. I might rewrite this part of the script a little bit. Then we'll have you and then your sister up."

"Sure," I said, relieved that the problem wasn't with

me. Then I realized a whole different problem; Emma was nowhere to be seen.

Emma wasn't here yet. And she was going to have go on at any time!

Emma

Eighteen

IN THE LOBBY OF SHIRA'S STUDIO

I paced back and forth in the studio lobby, waiting for Dad. Shira's mom was pacing nearby, waiting for Shira to come out of her audition. Jessica was filing her nails.

Brzzzzt.

I checked my phone. It was only Mason.

"Mason!" I said. "You have got to stop texting me."

"I did stop," Mason said, looking at me all innocent. "I requested a video chat instead."

Aaargh!

Why wasn't he in school doing something productive for a change? Why did he have to bother me when I had so much on my mind? Wait a minute. . . .

"Mason," I said. "Why aren't you in school?"

"I'm in my mom's office." He frowned. "Got in trouble with my teacher. And my gym teacher. And my—"

"Stop!" I said. "You're in your mom's office? In the middle school? In *my* middle school?"

"Yeah, are you gonna yell at me too? Cuz I—"

"No, no!" I said. "Not at all. First, tell me, is your mother there? I mean, Counselor Case. Is she with you?"

"Nah, she left me here to get us some lunch. I hope your cafeteria has better food than ours, cuz—"

"Shush," I interrupted him, thinking fast. "How would you like to help me?"

"What's in it for me?" he asked quickly.

I looked straight into my screen at his freckled, eight-year-old face.

"Cash," I said. "Cold, hard money."

"I'm in," he said. "What do I have to do?"

I gave him instructions on writing a short note to Ox—from me—and directions to Ox's locker.

"If you get caught," I finished, "say you're lost and ask where the boys' room is."

"Oh, I won't get caught," Mason said. "Trust me."

I have no choice, I thought. And shut off my phone.

"I've never seen you lose track of time before," Dad said as he walked into the studio lobby. "I'm very proud of you for taking the time to help someone else."

"Well, Shira is a kinesthetic learner. She learns better by moving, so we had to do some dance moves to memorize things. And as you know, my dance skills are zero but Shira nailed it. I'll bet her audition was awesome," I said. And yes, I felt proud of myself too.

"But now we better hurry to make it to your shoot," Dad said. We went down some stairs and out toward the sidewalk, when suddenly a golf cart with a big studio logo pulled up alongside us.

"Would you like a ride?" The studio golf cart driver asked us.

"Yes, please!" I said. Excellent. This would help me get to the studio so much faster. Dad and I climbed onto the golf cart.

"Studio Three, please," Dad said.

Then my video chat rang.

"It's Secret Agent Mason," Mason whispered loudly. "I'm having a problem with my mission. This girl won't let me in Ox's locker. Identify yourself."

He swiveled the camera so I could see a random girl on the screen.

"It's not Ox's locker," the girl said. "It's *my* locker. I told you that."

"She's breaking into Ox's locker!" Mason said. "She's a criminal! I have to tell my mom and get this girl thrown out of school!"

"Oh my gosh, I am not breaking into anybody's locker," the girl insisted into the phone. "This is my locker and this little child is driving me crazy."

"Sorry about him," I said into the phone. "That doesn't look like the right locker. Ox has a green locker; that one looks white."

Then I saw the number on the locker: 273. The wrong number.

"Mason," I said. "That's the wrong locker. Ox's is number two-seventy-*seven*."

Just then I heard the class bell ring. I couldn't hear what Mason said but I could read his lips on the screen: *Talk louder. I can't hear you.*

"Seven! SEVEN, NOT THREE!" I yelled. Mason gave me the thumbs-up on the screen and then looked panicked.

"Aw, man!" he said. "My dad is coming down the hall!"

His face disappeared from my screen. I hoped that

Mason didn't get in trouble with Coach. I really hoped he could get Ox's note into Ox's locker. But right now, I knew I had to focus on other things. I hoped I could get to Studio 3 on time to film the commercial without them even missing me. The golf cart zoomed through the streets of the studio lots.

And then suddenly the golf cart slowed down, and we were under attack by . . .

I looked at Dad, but he was busy texting and hadn't noticed the . . .

ZOMBIES!

I screamed.

Dad and the golf cart driver jumped in their seats.

"Are you okay?" Dad, who had been busy texting, looked up. And then he went, "Whoa! Zombies!"

"I hear there are one hundred extras for this zombie scene," the driver said.

Silly me! Of course, it was for a movie shoot. I felt a little foolish as my heart stopped racing. Whew. Hollywood could certainly make things look realistic.

Yes, a crowd of zombies was walking right in front of and behind our cart, crossing a street. Some had missing limbs, some were bleeding, and all of them had terrible expressions on their faces as they looked at me.

Even though I knew it was just makeup and costumes, the people crossing in front of me looked seriously creepy. Suddenly Payton's greasy hair didn't seem like such a bad look.

"Sorry for screaming," I called up to the front. "I was lost in thought and forgot where we were."

"Well, now I know why they cast your daughter in *Zombies Two*," the driver said. "That's some scream."

One zombie waved at me and I waved back. You don't see that every day.

After the zombies passed by, our golf cart started to move forward.

"I don't recognize any of this area." Dad looked around. "Maybe we're taking the long way around because of the zombie filming."

I shrugged. All of the buildings looked pretty much the same except for the numbers on them. But when the golf cart pulled up and the driver said that we were here, I saw the number seven.

"Can you point us in the right direction to walk to Studio Three?" Dad asked.

"Studio Three?" The driver turned around, looking puzzled. "I thought you had changed it to Studio Seven?"

Dad and I looked at each other blankly.

"You were calling to me, 'Seven! Seven, not Three!'" the driver insisted.

I scrolled through my (near-photographic) brain recall and that's when it dawned on me: He must've heard me shouting to Mason that the locker number was not three, but seven.

"I'm so sorry, I was talking on the phone," I told the driver. "How far away is Studio Three? I'm supposed to be filming a commercial at Studio Three."

"On the other side of the lot," the driver said. "It's a long walk, so I'll be happy to give you a ride that way. "So you're not here to be in the zombie movie? With a scream like that, I would've thought you'd be a shoo-in," the driver said.

Oh, this was not good. I frantically texted Payton that I was going to be late.

"Hang on to the handrails," the driver said. "I'm going to make this baby fly."

The golf cart zipped off toward Studio Three. I held on tight, and I held my breath, hoping I'd get there in time.

Nineteen

ON THE CORRECT STUDIO SET

Nooooo! I reread Emma's text message, hoping I'd read it wrong. She'd gone to Studio 7? Emma, messing up the number? Emma, the mathlete champion who practically never got a number wrong in her life?

It was probably Dad's fault.

But it didn't matter whose fault it was! Any minute they were going to call Emma to the set! And if she wasn't there, who knew what they'd do? Everything was going so perfectly and I felt like I was a professional actor, just like I dreamed. But who knew how mad they would be if Emma held up the filming. I knew that wasting time meant wasting money and the whole crew's time.

I felt like I was going to cry.

"I need to get your sister ready. Where is she?" Jean-Marie came up to me. Then she looked closer. "Are you rubbing your eyes? Better not let Lesly see that you're smearing her hard work on your makeup."

Then she looked closer at me.

"Oh, honey, are you crying? What's the matter? Can I help?"

I looked over at Zoe. She was talking to Ashlynn, and I definitely didn't want Ashlynn to know about any of this. I'd have to trust Jean-Marie to help me.

"My sister was helping somebody else with her audition on another lot and Dad went out to get her," I babbled. "But they got lost or something and Emma isn't here to get ready for her shoot."

"I see in my directions that your sister is supposed to have clean, shiny hair again," Jean-Marie said.

"Yes, it's the scene where she says, 'Shiny, shiny, shiny,' and whips her hair around."

"So you know her lines and what she's supposed to do?" Jean-Marie said. "Well, Twin Number Two—"

"I'm Twin Number One," I interrupted, pointing to my greasy head.

"Why hold up the shoot?" she continued cheerfully.

"Come on, Twin Number TWO, we're going to give you clean, shiny hair."

"You think I should go on as Emma?" I gasped.

"Never hold up a shoot if there's a way to avoid it." She smiled. "Plus, I don't want her in trouble. She helped me with my exam; I'll help her back. I'll tell the makeup artist to do your makeup like hers and if Emma doesn't make it in time, we'll cover for her. Now let's go."

She whisked me off to the hair chair and gave me the fastest shampoo of my life. As she blow-dried my hair, I texted Emma.

Janitor's closet time 911!

That was our code word for a twin switch. I texted more.

I'm doing your scene. I'm now u.

"So glad I got this new blow-dryer prototype," Jean-Marie said. "It's not even on the market. Watch this."

Jean-Marie gave me the fastest blow-dry of my life. She fluffed and ta-da! I looked at myself in the mirror and smiled. My hair had gone from greasy to gorgeous!

"Thanks!" I hugged her and saw I had a new text.

k. on my way. "P"

"Twin Number Two!" the assistant director called out. "On set!"

I took a deep breath and channeled my inner Emma. Twin #2 was about to be shiny, shiny, and shiny. Twin Switch: Hollywood was under way.

And . . . action! I went into full-on Emma mode. She had excellent posture, so I stood up a little straighter. She was a little less bouncy than me and definitely less squealy. I went out onto the set and hit my mark.

"Teen Sheen, scene three, take one." The clapboard clapped.

"And . . . action!"

"Shiny, shiny, shiny!" I whipped my hair around and smiled.

"Cut!" The director smiled back. "Well that was perfect. You seem nice and relaxed today, Twin Number Two. Let's shoot that a couple times just to be safe, but do exactly what you just did.

So I did.

"Excellent—your smile was nice and natural, and your hair sure is shiny," the director said.

"Emma, you can take five while your sister shoots the next scene," the assistant director told me.

Eep. I raced over to Jean-Marie, who was holding my phone out to me. I texted my sister.

Where are you?

Lot 4. Coming! Emma texted back.

But not soon enough. Jean-Marie saw the look on my face.

"Can you give me an extra minute to work on Twin Number One?" she called out. "I need to grease her hair a little more."

"Okay," the assistant director told her. "So you have a few minutes."

"Let's do it," Jean-Marie whispered to me. We raced past the crew, the craft services area, and back to the hair area. I quickly ducked into the changing closet and switched Emma's costume for mine. I jumped into the chair and Jean-Marie leaned my head back over the sink and poured the greasy stuff all over me again.

I was back to being greasy me, not shiny Emma. (That still didn't sound right to me.)

I ran back to the set with Jean-Marie behind me. "Go, Twin Number One," she said.

I hit my mark and . . .

"ACTION!"

"I have to try Teen Sheen shampoo!" I said, holding up the bottle of shampoo. They made me do three more takes and then I had it.

"Now we need Twin Number Two for her last individual shot," the assistant director announced.

I raced over to Jean-Marie and checked my phone. *Nothing. Emma, where are you? Not here, apparently.*

"Can I have two minutes to shine Twin Number One's hair? I know this is a close-up, and I can get it perfect," Jean-Marie told him.

"Let's take five," the director said.

Jean-Marie and I knew what we had to do. And fast. We raced back to her area, dunked my head in the sink for another fast shampoo and blow-dry. I threw on the blue T-shirt and raced back to the set. Jean-Marie whispered to me, "I'll go see if I can intercept your sister."

I was panting and out of breath at this point. But boy, did my hair look good.

"Twin Number Two, we are thinking of switching it up a bit. Do you know how to do a cartwheel?" the assistant director asked me. "We're thinking of adding one in because that will show off the movement of your hair."

"Yes," I said. "Yes, I do."

"Excellent. I have to say, I'm very impressed with you today, Twin Number Two. You are just what we needed."

Yes, yes, I was. Because Emma totally did not know

how to do a cartwheel. But I did! And I could be Twin #2 cartwheeling away!

I went and I cartwheeled my brains out through nine takes.

And on the tenth, I was mid-cartwheel when I saw an upside face of . . . Emma! My sister was here! And she was wearing my T-shirt and sweats, standing casually at the side of the set with Jean-Marie. I broke out into a grin. I saw her give me the thumbs-up as I flipped right side up.

"Cut!" the director called out. "Love the natural smile at the end! Let's take two minutes and then film the final scenes with both of you ladies."

Both of us! Me and Emma, together where we were supposed to be. Phew!

I half stumbled off the set, dizzy and seeing double from all of the cartwheeling. It was like seeing two Emmas. Or two Paytons. Or . . . both of us. Whoa. Freaky.

"Good job, Emma," Emma grinned at me. "Twin Number Two! Heh, I said 'number two'! Oh, that reminds me, I have to check on Mission Mason as soon as I'm done."

"I don't even want to know," I said.

"I'm just relieved I didn't have to cartwheel," Emma told me.

"Girls, I think we need to fix both of your hair, if you catch my drift. You can tell me about it later," Jean-Marie looked at us pointedly and then down at our outfits.

Then she winked. We had to twin-switch our clothes! And go back to our real selves.

Twin #1! And Twin #2! Together! We made our way past the crew and past the craft services table, where I made a quick pitstop.

"Hi, Dad!"

"I was just getting a little snack and then heading over to watch the filming," Dad said. "Are you girls almost up yet?"

Emma and I looked at each other and laughed.

"We have to get ready and then we're doing our last scene," I told him. "See you there."

"Let's wrap this thing up, Twin Number Two." I smiled at Emma.

"Let's do it, Twin Number One—*and Two*," Emma said back.

Twenty

IN THE CORRECT STUDIO

Jean-Marie did our hair and we headed back toward the set. The assistant director told us to wait by the side while they finished setting things up.

I was really proud of Payton for saving the day. And I was really happy for her, because it looked like she was having so much fun doing it. Payton really seemed to love everything about this acting gig. As for me, I had to admit I was ready for it to be over with. Some of it I found boring. And I was seriously tired of having my hair brushed and being poked with makeup brushes.

Payton, however, loved the pampering. Especially

since she didn't have to have a greasy head anymore. And she got a wardrobe change.

"Ta-da!" she twirled around. She was wearing an outfit that matched mine, but the shirt was bright purple. The tank was fuchsia and the skirt was still yellow.

"Blindingly bright," she whispered. "But better than sweatpants and greasy hair!"

I saw Ashlynn come onto the set and glare at me. I was also seriously tired of Ashlynn.

I looked at Payton. She was in her zone, rehearsing her lines for the next scene. I tried to block Ashlynn from her so Payton could stay in her happy acting zone. But Ashlynn marched up to us.

"So are you happy now?" Ashlynn asked, putting her hands on her hips and glaring at us.

"What are you talking about, Ashlynn?" I sighed.

"Is this why you were all over my handler last night, Payton?" Ashlynn held out her phone and I could see the picture of Payton with Dustin Weaver on it.

"Oh, you saw that." Payton sighed. "Yeah, isn't it crazy?"

"Crazy? Nice try, acting all innocent," Ashlynn said. "You knew that Zoe is one of the best publicists in

Hollywood. Your sucking up to her worked."

"What are you talking about?" I said. "You know Payton didn't know Dustin Weaver."

"What I do know is that after Payton was monopolizing my handler, my handler told her she should go check out the celebrities close-up. And then Payton just happens to 'fall' into Dustin's arms, resulting in a romantic embrace? I smell a setup," Ashlynn accused.

"And I smell something delusional," I said. "As in you."

"Although it's pretty impressive that you got to spin the story as a romantic date," Ashlynn said, "I wouldn't have thought you two had it in you."

"We would never do that!" Payton burst out.

"Why would we even do that?" I asked. "That's ridiculous."

"Why would you even *do* that?" Ashlynn snorted. "What a great way to get publicity: pretend to be in a relationship with a celebrity. Plus you get to have something to impress your little friends from home, which I'm sure doesn't happen very often."

I rolled my eyes, but before I could respond, Payton did. And Payton was really, really upset. *Uh-oh.*

"We *don't* want our friends to think we had a date with Dustin Weaver! We both have boys we like!" Payton blurted out. "And the boys don't know which one of us was in the picture!"

"Stop talking, Payton," I muttered. But Ashlynn now had all the ammunition that she needed.

"Oh." She smiled. "I remember something about that when you were in New York. You and your hick school lizard boys. Well, then your little scheme backfired. It probably has them pretty upset with you, Dustin Weaver's Mystery Love," she said, turning to Payton.

Then she turned to me.

"Or are *you* Dustin Weaver's Mystery Love?"

And that's when she got to me. I had been trying to ignore everything Ashlynn was saying since it was so ludicrous. But . . . what if Ox really was upset with me? I couldn't stand it anymore. I had to know if Mason had gotten the note to Ox and if Ox had gotten back to me yet. Jean-Marie was holding my phone for me, so I decided I needed a quick check. I was about to pull Payton to come with me—and keep her away from Ashlynn. But the assistant director called her first.

"Twin Number One!" she called out, and waved Payton onto the set.

"Is that the real Twin Number One, or are you

switching places again?" Ashlynn asked evilly. I hurried away from her and over to Jean-Marie.

"May I check my phone?" But before Jean-Marie could give it to me, I got called to the set too. I tried to put both Ashlynn and Ox out of my head as the director gave us our instructions for the final shoot. We just had to say our lines, and this time Payton would toss the shampoo bottle to me.

"Teen Sheen, scene four, take one!" The clapboard clapped.

"And . . . action!"

"Wow! Teen Sheen Shampoo really works!" Payton said. And to give her credit, she didn't seem to let Ashlynn bother her at all. She flipped her hair back and forth and gave a dazzling smile.

I, however, could see Ashlynn out of the corner of my eye. She was holding up something and waving it in my direction. It was my . . . phone? Ashlynn had my cell phone and was looking at it. And then she looked up and smiled. Wait, was she reading my texts? Was there a text from Ox? And if there was, did it explain why she was smiling? If Ashlynn was smiling, that meant it was something bad for me.

Did he think that was really me with Dustin Weaver?

Did Ox text that he was disappointed in me? Was it over between the two of us, whatever the two of us was?!?!

"Hey, don't steal my Teen Sheen." I growled my line. Payton flinched and took a step back.

"Cut!" the director yelled.

"Twin Number Two, can you say that line a little less . . . angrily?" the director said to me. "Yes, you're supposed to feel attached to your Teen Sheen shampoo but it's supposed to be a little humorous. Not like you're going to harm your twin."

Oops. I'd accidentally let my anger at Ashlynn escape. I, famous for not showing emotion under pressure—for example, during elections for sixth-grade class president when my opponent made farting noises throughout my entire speech and I stayed calm. (And I won.)

"Sorry," I apologized. After all the times I'd told Payton not to let Ashlynn get to her, I finally succumbed to Ashlynn myself.

"There is a hair emergency!" Jean-Marie suddenly called out. "A hair out of place! Twin Number Two, may I see you for a second?"

The director broke for the hair emergency. I went over to Jean-Marie.

"There's no hair emergency. You look like you needed

191

a moment," she whispered in my ear. "What's up?"

"Does Ashlynn have my phone?" I whispered to her.

"I left it on the chair." She tilted her head toward a chair and then she frowned. "Wait, where did it go?"

I looked at the set and saw they were blotting my sister's face. I walked up to Ashlynn.

"Give me my phone," I demanded.

"I was just being helpful," she said innocently. "I didn't want anybody to steal it. Besides, you didn't get any text messages, if that's what you're wondering."

That's exactly what I had been wondering. She'd been playing mind games all along. And I'd fallen for it. Ashlynn handed me my phone. I was about to say something to her that I might regret later when my phone buzzed. I looked down and saw a new text from . . . Ox!

I had a dilemma. Should I read it now? But what if it was bad news and distracted me from our commercial shoot? I just couldn't do that to Payton, or risk messing up our job. Logically, I should just walk away and read it later.

But I opened it.

Hey! How's Hollywood, TV star? I'm home sick from school today. Bad cold. Achoo! Did you know in ancient times they thought sneezing let the devil *in your mouth?*

That's why they say "Bless you."—I miss you, too.

A dazzling smile broke out across my face. Ox hadn't heard a thing about Dustin Weaver! And I'd be able to fill them in before he did!!! I texted back.

Did you know the Tasmanian devil is the mammal with the strongest bite-force quotient? Funny story about Payton and a website to tell you—all a fake. Payton fell on a celeb—and funny scandal made up! So disregard. Holly wood is HollyWEIRD. Feel better.

I hit the send button. Hurrah!! Everything was fine with me and Ox! Better than fine! Dazzlingly fine! I felt so much better now. Oh yeah. Emma Mills was back in action.

"Excuse me," I said to the meaningless gnat that was Ashlynn. "I have a commercial to film. Step aside."

Jean-Marie glared at Ashlynn as I handed Jean-Marie my phone for safekeeping. I practically skipped out to the set.

"Ox misses me," I sang out to my sister. She mouthed back, *Yay!*

And it was time to film our final scene!

"Teen Sheen, scene four, take two!"

"And . . . action!" the director called out.

"Wow! Teen Sheen shampoo really works!" Payton

said. She flipped her hair back and forth and gave a seriously dazzling smile.

"Hey, don't steal my Teen Sheen." I smiled at her
and added a wink. And my not-just-for-TV dazzling
smile.

That was when Payton was supposed to gently toss
me the bottle of shampoo, I would catch it and hold it
up, and we'd say our last line together.

Except it didn't exactly work that way. I don't know
if Payton was still frustrated with Ashlynn, or if she just
didn't have my water polo tossing skills, but when she
threw the shampoo bottle it flew over my shoulder and
went flying . . . flying . . . and . . .

BONK!

It smacked Ashlynn. A direct hit on the side of her
head.

Twenty-one

POST-COMMERCIAL, OUTSIDE THE STUDIO

"And then it was like, *Bonk!*" I pretended to get hit in the side of the head, making my hair fly out just like Ashlynn's. And we both laughed. Obviously the fake shampoo bottle was lightweight, like a beach ball, so it didn't hurt her. But it had hurt her pride.

"And that noise she made was really funny," I said. "'Oof!' It made everyone look at her."

"And not in a way she wanted," Emma added.

Perhaps we should have felt bad about Ashlynn's embarrassment, but no. It was poetic justice. Karma. She had tried to mess with the Mills Twins.

So, heh heh heh.

We were waiting outside the studio for our car. We had changed out of our wardrobe, and we were back to being us. Well, we were back to being me, since we were both wearing my clothes. I was wearing a white shirt and an orange skirt, and Emma was wearing a plaid shirt, denim shorts, and brown leather flip-flops. And . . .

"I just realized that the tank top you're wearing under your shirt is one of Ashlynn's Summer Slave tanks," I said. "Ack. Hide it. She might finish filming anytime and we'll see her."

"You know what?" Emma said. "I don't care and neither do you." She took off the button-down and stood proudly in the bright blue tank top that had little sequins on the back. And I realized Emma was right. I finally didn't care.

Emma's phone rang.

"It's Shira," Emma said. "Hello?"

I could hear voices talking and Emma started to smile. She told Shira where we were and then muted the phone.

"Dad!" she said. "Shira wanted to know if she can come over and tell us something really quick. She's just over at Studio Five."

"Sure," he said. "We have the car and driver all day and there's no rush."

We didn't have to wait long before a golf cart zipped up and deposited Shira, Jessica, and their mom in front of us.

"How'd it go?" I asked.

"Awesome! Thanks to your sister." She beamed.

"Neither of us got the part," Jessica grumbled.

"But I got a callback! So after the first audition with you, Emma, I got to go into the second round!" Shira said. "That's never happened before, and they told me that I was one of their top picks."

"You really boosted her confidence," their mother said. "We greatly appreciate the help that Emma gave Shira today."

Emma shuffled, embarrassed by the gratitude.

"Well, we'll see you back at the apartments, I hope," Shira said. "When do you all leave?"

"Tomorrow morning," I said. It seemed way too soon.

"Well, if we don't see you, thanks again," Shira said. "Friend me."

"Do you guys have any other auditions here before you leave?" Jessica asked in her nosy manner.

Shira rolled her eyes and dragged Jessica away.

"Well, ladies," our dad said, "I didn't realize we would have so much free time left. What would you like to do?"

The car pulled up to the curb.

"I don't know—" I started to say, and then I saw Ashlynn and Zoe coming out of the studio door. "Quick, jump in before they see us."

But it was too late. Zoe spotted us and motioned for us to wait for them. Ashlynn didn't look too happy about it, but she came over too. Probably thinking we were going after her handler again. But no, we were just going . . . away from the studio and the entertainment business. *Sigh.*

"I'm glad I caught you," Zoe said. "Do you all have plans yet for the evening?"

"We were just about to discuss that," my father said. "Maybe a little sightseeing, but we're not sure."

"Would you like to go to see the filming of a new TV show?" Zoe asked. "It's going to be on the Tween Channel."

What? Emma and I looked at each other, excited.

"But sightseeing is a good idea," Ashlynn butted in. "You can totally do that instead."

"We have these tickets to be in the audience because of Emma." Zoe held up the tickets. Then she looked sternly at Ashlynn. "So if Emma doesn't go, you don't go either, Ashlynn."

"Fine." Ashlynn rolled her eyes.

"Because of me?" Emma asked. "I'm confused."

"Jean-Marie's boyfriend is a production assistant on the new show that's filming." Zoe smiled. "She got us these tickets to thank you for helping her with study tips, Emma. So do you want to go be in the studio audience for the filming of a new show?"

Emma and I looked at each other.

"Yes!" we both screamed.

While Zoe and Dad worked out the ride situation, Emma and I jumped around excitedly. Ashlynn was on the phone. We couldn't help but hear her when she started yelling.

"No, I didn't get any more auditions, Mother," she said. "I was busy working all day. Now I'm going to see a show getting filmed. . . . What do you mean, a waste of time? I want to have a little bit of fun."

Emma and I looked at each other. That sounded intense.

"Fine, I'll try to get *on* the show okay? Now, good-bye."

She hung up the phone. Then she looked at us. "I know you heard that. My mother is annoyed at Zoe for wasting audition time."

"Ashlynn, I'm happy to take you wherever your mother wants you to go," Zoe said. "Do you want me to speak to her?"

Suddenly Ashlynn looked really pitiful.

"No, she was busy getting her nails done. Too busy to come out here with me, so it's her problem. I want to go see this show filming," she said, grimly determined. But then she perked up. "But our seats better be in the front row. Maybe I can get discovered."

Twenty-two

IN LINE FOR TV SHOW

The line to go into the studio snaked around the whole building. All of the kids looked excited, and some of the parents looked excited too.

All we knew was that it was a segment called Brainy Mania and it would air on the new Tween Channel in between some of Payton's favorite shows.

"What kind of name is 'Brainy Mania,' anyway?" Ashlynn whined. Ashlynn had whined during the whole car ride. And then once we arrived, she whined about having to stand in line instead of going in a VIP entrance, she whined when they told her she had to turn off her cell phone, and she whined about other things that I don't even know because I tuned her out completely.

"This is seriously cool," Payton said to me. "Just think, when the show airs, we'll be able to say we were here!"

Payton, like me, had finally managed to tune Ashlynn out as well.

"Maybe this show will be a huge hit and we will be able to say that we saw it before anybody else," I replied.

"It better be a good show," Ashlynn muttered.

"I heard it's a trivia show," a kid behind us piped up.

I expected Ashlynn to whine about that, too, but to my surprise she perked up.

"Trivia?" she said. "I'm fabulous at trivia."

I snorted.

"I am." Ashlynn looked offended.

"You are excellent at whining, having a sense of entitlement, and trying to ruin people," I said. "I don't believe you are excellent at trivia."

Ashlynn knew a challenge when she heard one.

"Try me." Ashlynn narrowed her eyes at me.

And the challenge was on.

Ashlynn and I started to zing back and forth. When the kids in front of us turned around to watch and then started to cheer, other people started to check out what we were doing. Soon a crowd of kids was gathered around us.

"What is the colorful atmospheric heating phenomenon *efecto invernadero*?" Ashlynn asked the first question.

"The greenhouse effect," Emma said. "What element is number ninety-nine on the periodic table?"

"Einstenium," Ashlynn shot back. The small crowd applauded. "What breed is the smallest living dog?"

"A chihuahua," I answered correctly. "Named Heaven Sent Brandy."

"What is going on here?" I heard a woman ask Payton.

"They're having a trivia-off," Payton explained. "Right now they're tied."

We were tied. Whoever missed a question would lose. And it was not going to be me, I decided. I gave Ashlynn my best "take you down" game face, the one that even threw Jazmine James off sometimes. Ashlynn shot me a game face that was as good, if not better. Whoa, that girl was serious competition.

I had underestimated her. She got two more right, as did I. And then I posed a question to her and her face crumpled. She took a deep breath and then:

"And the answer is . . . the dung beetle?" Ashlynn said.

"Wrong! The *snout* beetle!" I shouted. "The answer is the snout beetle, also known as the weevil!"

The crowd cheered for me. Ashlynn stamped her foot on the ground as I danced around her in a victory dance. Yes! The winner was ME!

"Go, Emma!" I heard my sister cheer. Woot! Victory for me! The crowd clapped and went back to their places in line.

"Please stop the awkward dance," Ashlynn said to me.

"You were a surprisingly worthy opponent," I told Ashlynn, stopping my victory dance but not my dazzling smile!

"Grumble," Ashlynn grumbled.

"Emma." Dad came closer from where he'd been standing off to the side with Zoe and the lady who had asked Payton what was going on. Now they all came back up to us. "This is an assistant producer on the show we're about to see."

"Oh, I'm sorry," I said. "We didn't mean to be disruptive."

"No need for apologies," the woman said. "In fact,

it's the opposite. You both were very compelling and entertaining. I wish I had spots for both of you but I only have one spot left, and I guess it's only fair that I invite the winner of your competition to be on ours."

She looked at me, then Ashlynn. I didn't know what she was talking about.

"I'd like to know if you would like to be a contestant on Brainy Mania," she said. "We are bringing in a couple teens to be on the show."

"Now?" I couldn't believe what I was hearing.

"If you want to do it, honey, you may," Dad said. "Payton, are you okay staying with Zoe and Ashlynn so Emma and I can go in?"

"Sure," Payton said. "That's awesome."

"Yeah, awesome," Ashlynn said. "Not."

Too bad, so sad. But Ashlynn really did look sad, so I put on my good-sport hat.

"Sorry, Ashlynn," I said. "You were a solid competitor. If you want to go onstage, well, I know you like to be there more than I do . . ."

"Are you offering to let me take your place?" she looked surprised.

Payton looked at me like I was crazy. But really, I'd had my share of the stage for one day.

But Ashlynn shook her head.

"I'm no understudy." She tossed her hair. "You got the role fair and square. So just go. Oh, and you better win."

Payton and I looked at each other, surprised.

"Go, Emma!" Payton said. "Go!"

So I went.

Twenty-three

STUDIO AUDIENCE OF A REAL, LIVE TV GAME SHOW

Emma was going to be on a TV game show!

"Well that was certainly very exciting," Zoe said. "I'm impressed with Emma. I'm also impressed with you two."

"What did we do?" Ashlynn asked. "We didn't get picked and we're stuck here in line with everybody else."

She wrinkled up her nose.

"But you were very gracious when you didn't get picked." Zoe looked pointedly at Ashlynn. "Well, up until that last sentence, anyway. You've also both been waiting patiently. Graciousness and patience are qualities that help in this business, which is a lot of waiting around and of course a good deal of rejection. You've experienced a taste of it."

I liked that compliment. Ashlynn looked a little less cranky, so she must have too. Then Ashlynn's phone rang.

"It's my manager. Maybe I've been cast in a game show too," she said. Ashlynn went off and stood away from the line a bit.

I looked at my phone and realized that everyone at home was out of school. I could tell them about everything! And now about Emma being a contestant on a TV show!

I pulled out my phone and saw that Tess and Quinn were available to video chat. I waited as their little faces popped up on my screen.

"Payton!" they both said, waving at the screen.

"You guys are not going to believe this," I started telling them. "Guess where Emma is?"

"Secretly eloping with Dustin Weaver?" Tess joked. "She better not be—he's all mine!"

"Then you'll be happy to know she isn't. But you guys, she's going to be on a TV game show!" I explained to them how Emma had gotten picked to go on this new show. They both went a little crazy.

"You guys are so Hollywood," Quinn said.

"Check out the scene." I held up my phone and moved it slowly around so they could see everything going on around me.

"That's so cool," Quinn said. "Hey, is that girl waving at you?"

Hmm. It looked like Ashlynn was waving me over. I took a few steps toward her and then I heard Tess call my name from the phone.

"Payton, maybe the screen is just blurry, but that girl looks exactly like the girl from New York City who tried to sabotage the Drama Geckos!"

I could see Tess squinting at her computer screen up close. I realized I hadn't yet mentioned Ashlynn was here.

"Long story. I'll tell you about it when I get back," I said. "Yes, that's her. She's filming the commercial too."

"Well don't go over to her, don't get sucked in," Tess warned. "She might be waving at you to sabotage you again."

"Also a long story, but I think I've got her under control," I said. Although Ashlynn looked like she was kind of out of control herself. She was waving at me with both hands now.

"I better go over, but I'll bring you guys with me for

backup protection." I laughed. "You can be my witnesses if evil occurs."

I walked up to Ashlynn, holding my phone up toward her.

"Say hi to my friends from home," I said to Ashlynn.

"Wait!" Tess gasped. "It *is* the girl from New York! That girl pushed a puppy!"

I'd forgotten about that. Ashlynn suddenly froze. She turned bright red. And then she leaned close to the phone, taking me by surprise.

"I had great remorse for that," Ashlynn said. "I have since put in more than seventy-five hours at the dog shelter, walking dogs and giving them the love they deserve. I raised more than six hundred and fifty dollars for blankets for them to snuggle in. So far."

"Oh," I heard Quinn say. "Wow."

"I also just sent Bebe, Barbra, and LeaMichele an assortment of dog chewies and darling outfits at their new home," Ashlynn said.

"Okay then." Tess sounded somewhat appeased.

"And now, *this* is what I called you over to see." Ashlynn pointed over to the long black town car that was waiting at the curb of the studio lot. A door was opening.

"What is it?" I asked.

"Just turn your phone toward that black car," Ashlynn said. "Trust me."

Trust Ashlynn? Well, there was a first for everything. I turned the phone to the car and that's when I heard the screams.

Screams from the crowd of kids waiting in line. Screams from the moms waiting with their kids. And I heard Tess and Quinn erupt into screams too. Because the guy getting out of the car was: Enrique Rico! Yes, the movie star. The hot, scorching-hot-with-a-smoldering-gaze movie star. And he was right there, right in front of us, steps away from me.

"Get closer, Payton!" Quinn squealed. I inched my way closer, and Ashlynn was right with me.

"Look at that hair," Tess gasped.

"Look at his eyes," Quinn oohed.

"Look at his muscles," I sighed. I gazed at his sheer hotness as he got out of the car, flanked by huge body-guards.

And then he walked closer and closer, shielded by the bodyguards but still waving to the screaming crowd. I held up the cell phone so Tess and Quinn could see him too. And as he walked by I swear he looked right at me and said, "Hello."

Ashlynn and I looked at each other and screamed. Tess and Quinn screamed.

The people in front of us screamed as he continued walking past them and into the studio.

AHHHHHHHHHH!

"Now that was a celebrity sighting," Ashlynn said proudly. "When I saw that car, my star radar went off and I was right. Was I right or was I right? And did you see how he said hello to me?"

"No, he said hello to me," I said. "And I have witnesses, right guys?"

"No, he was definitely saying hi to us," Quinn said. "Tess and I saw him look right into the phone at us."

"Yup." Tess nodded. We all laughed. Then I saw another one of my friends pop up and request a chat. It was Nick! His face showed up on the screen next to Tess and Quinn.

"Oh my gosh, oh my gosh, Nick, you won't believe who we just saw!" Tess and Quinn screamed.

"Dustin Dreamy?" Nick asked.

"No, that was so yesterday," Quinn squealed. "Enrique Rico!"

Then we all shrieked again.

"Oh my gosh, he was so cute," Tess squealed. "And

he walked right by Payton and said hello to her!"

"He's so hot, I might faint," Quinn said.

"Wow, that's pretty hot." Nick grinned. "Payton, are you still standing?"

"Quinn, I think we'd better sign off and let these two chat in private." Tess winked at me.

"I'm only kidding," Nick protested. "Although I did notice both of your celebrity sightings happened to be quote 'cute' guys."

"That's right." Ashlynn stuck her head in front of mine on the screen. "We're attracting all the hotties here in Hollywood, so you better step up your game if you want to keep Payton at home."

"Ashlynn!" I shushed her. Yikes! "Ignore her, Nick."

"Payton knows I'm not into playing games, whoever you are." Nick was grinning.

"I'm Ashlynn," she announced. "Soon to be a Hollywood celebrity, and everybody will know who I am. Talk to me now before I have security who will block you."

She struck a pose.

"Okay, enough flirting," I told her, and swung the camera back to my face.

"Do I know that girl from somewhere?" Nick asked. "She looks familiar."

"I'll explain later," I told him. "I've got so much to tell you. Like how right now Emma is about to be a contestant on a game show."

"Awesome," Nick said.

And then the line started moving forward. It was time to go in to the show!

"The line is moving! I have to go, but I'll talk to you later. And . . . I can't wait to see you," I said. Ashlynn started making kissing noises next me.

"Dustin Weaver is going to be very jealous," Ashlynn said.

"Oh, shush," I said to her as we rejoined Zoe at the door.

"Did you girls see Enrique Rico?" she asked us. "I'm swooning!"

"You should have given him your business card," I said. "I'm sure he'd be more fun to handle than Ashlynn."

"Hey!" Ashlynn said, but you could tell the Enrique sighting had put her in a good—well, good for Ashlynn, anyway—mood.

And just before we got to the door where we had to turn off our cell phones I quickly texted Ox about what Emma was doing. He texted back: *She told me. Cheer her on for me.*

I turned off my phone and we went in to our assigned seats. I was sitting next to the aisle on one side, then Ashlynn next to me and Zoe next to her.

We watched as a comedian warmed up the crowd with jokes. When he announced that the game show was about to start filming, everybody cheered. I looked around the room. It was a big room with a stage in the front that was half blocked by a red curtain. We had gotten really good seats on the floor.

"Welcome to . . . Brainy Mania!" An announcer's voice boomed through the room. "And I'm your host, Stewart!"

Hey! He played the funny and disturbing older brother on one of the Tween Channel's shows. We all cheered when we recognized him.

The monitors on the side of the stage blinked: APPLAUSE!

The audience obliged and applauded like crazy. Stewart explained the rules. Contestants had to answer questions and if they got them right they'd win prizes.

Ooh! Prizes! I hoped Emma would win something!

But then Stewart explained that when the contestants gave the wrong answer, they would have to meet their doom. A spotlight shone on the right side of the stage, but all we could see was the curtain.

And then they cut the filming for a break. Stewart got a makeup touch-up onstage and the crew ran around doing stuff.

"'Meet their doom'?" I was worried. "I don't want my sister to meet her doom!"

"She better win, then." Ashlynn shrugged, then looked at me. "Or buh-bye, Emma!"

"Easy, Ashlynn," Zoe said.

"Go, Zoe." I nodded. "Handle that Ashlynn for me, will you?"

"Hey!" Ashlynn grinned. "You don't expect me to not be a little bitter about her being up on the stage instead of me, do you? Then again, if she meets her doom that will take away some of the sting."

"I wonder when Emma will go on," I said. "I don't know how long I can stand the suspense."

And that's when it hit me. Emma was actually going to go up onto that stage and be faced with trivia questions, and possibly meet her doom! I suddenly felt very, very nervous for her. I used my twin telepathy to send her messages:

Go, Emma!

Don't worry about meeting your doom! Remember, it's just a kids show! How bad can the doom be, right? I think? Don't do that thing where you cross your eyes when you're trying to think of a hard answer!

Go, Emma!

"Are you ready for our first contestant on Brainy Mania?" Stewart yelled. "Audience, are you ready to see someone show their brains?"

The monitors flashed and everybody yelled along with him:

SHOW YOUR BRAINS!

"Our first contestant is . . . Emma!"

Oh my gosh! My sister was the first contestant! She walked onstage, turned toward the audience, and gave a slightly awkward wave.

Emma looked relaxed! She smiled and looked like she wasn't totally freaking out. But I was totally freaking out! Ahhhh!

"Ahhhhhh!" I screamed. "Go, Emma!"

"Go, Emma!" Ashlynn screamed from the seat next to me. I turned to her, surprised.

"What? You think I'm not going to cheer on your sister?" Ashlynn said, and then smiled. "Besides, she's good advertising for me. She is wearing my brand."

Huh?

"My tank top," Ashlynn explained. "I bet you thought I didn't notice she was wearing one of my hand-me-downs, Summer Slave."

Erg. My smiled dropped off my face.

"Oh, lighten up." Ashlynn elbowed me and smiled. "I designed that one myself, so your twin actually is showing some good taste for once. The sequins on the back are my fashion label logo. Fashlynn by Ashlynn is about to make its television debut!"

Twenty-four

GAME SHOW SET

Certainly, I was nervous and my adrenaline was pumping as I was called onto the stage. For one thing, I don't like to be onstage, under the spotlights. Unless it was for a competition where I could wield my academic knowledge like a sharp sword. But that was after hours and hours of preparation. I had zero preparation for this game show. I hadn't studied the competition, or the official rules, or the success tactics of previous years' winners.

Plus the wireless microphone clipped to my (Ashlynn's) tank top was scratchy.

However, I was slightly mollified by the fact that the

game show was called Brainy Mania. The motto was "Show your brains."

As long as you didn't take it literally—that would be gross—it sounded right up my alley.

Before the show, the backstage people had asked me some random trivia questions, from math to pop culture, and I got them all right. They asked me if I was comfortable onstage. (What the heck, I said yes). The only weird part was when they asked me what I thought of ooze.

That was the only question I didn't know the answer for. Ooze must be a new singer or actor . . . someone I hadn't heard of before.

I did have a flashback about the word "ooze." It was how I met Ox, in a way. Payton had spilled her cafeteria burrito on him and had called me freaking out that she had "oozed Ox."

Ox!

So when they asked me if I was okay with ooze, I smiled at the memory. "Ooze can be a great thing," I told them.

They seemed to be happy with that and made me . . .

Contestant #1. Number one! I'm #1! Woo-hoo!

"You're on in five." A man gestured to me and checked

that my microphone was on. "Four . . . three . . . two . . . one."

He guided me out to the stage where the host I'd met earlier was jumping around.

"Emma! Are you ready to show your brains?" Stewart asked me. The audience cheered for me.

For me! I knew my sister was out there somewhere, but I couldn't see a thing because of the lights shining onstage.

"Yes! I'm ready to show my brains!" I said, just like I'd been coached a few minutes ago backstage. I flashed my dazzling Teen Sheen shampoo smile. It was coming more naturally now.

They explained the rules. It was pretty simple. They'd ask me a question and if I got it right, exciting things would happen.

The audience cheered as I pumped my fist. Hey, this was fun. I was really working the crowd. This didn't happen in the spelling bee, where everyone was tense and not allowed to applaud.

I pumped my fist again and the audience went nuts again! I could get used to this.

"But Emma, if you get the answer wrong . . ." Stewart trailed off. "You will meet your doom."

My *what?* What happened if I got the answer wrong? My doom? They didn't tell me *that* backstage. I thought they just called another contestant up. Anyway, I planned to avoid that situation by winning, so perhaps it was moot.

"Excuse me, exactly what does happen if I get the answer wrong?" I asked politely.

"We have lots of surprises in store!" Stewart said, and the audience cheered. That did not quite answer my question. But then Stewart said it was time for me to start.

I shifted my brain into competition mode. This time there was no Jazmine James or her ilk to compete against. This time I was competing against myself. And I planned to win.

"First question," Stewart said. "Which continent has the most land area?"

No problemo. "The answer is Asia, which is seventeen-point-four million square miles."

"Correct!" Stewart shouted.

The audience went wild. Stewart jumped all over the stage, pumping his fist. Then suddenly—*bang!* Confetti cannons shot off and sprayed confetti all over the audience. Everyone was jumping up in their seats, and that's when I spotted Payton jumping up into one of the aisles.

Payton! I waved her way. Then the spotlight aimed back on me before I could see if she'd responded. *Okay, focus, Emma.*

"You got the first question correct! And that means you win a HelpLine pass! That means you can call somebody from the audience to help you with your answer to the next question!"

The audience cheered and chanted, "Show your brains!"

"Next question. The category is: Broadway Musicals!" Stewart said.

Okay, I'd just been to Broadway, but I didn't know trivia about it. As much as it pained me to do it, I knew what I had to do. And as much as I wanted my sister to have the chance to appear on television, I knew who I had to call on for this particular question.

"Do you want to call on a friend using your HelpLine?" Stewart asked.

Well, I needed a HelpLine, but I wouldn't exactly use the word "friend."

"This is not my specialty," I said. "I need help from an audience member: Ashlynn."

The camera crew ran through the audience and over to where Ashlynn was standing and waving her hands wildly. Her face showed up on the big screens throughout the studio. Ashlynn smoothed her hair down and put on her most actressy smile.

"Work together, you two! The question is: What inner-city gang musical was based on Shakespeare's *Romeo and Juliet*?"

"The answer is . . ." Ashlynn tossed her hair and built up suspense. *"West Side Story."*

"Yes," I agreed. *"West Side Story."*

"That is correct!" Stewart yelled, and the audience went wild. I clapped too, and mouthed *Good job* to Ashlynn, although I think she was too busy posing for the camera to notice. But then the camera moved to the side and there was Payton! Yay! Payton got to be on TV! *Hi, Payton!*

"Your bonus for getting that question correct is . . . the Brain Oozer!"

The whuh? Someone from the crew ran onto the stage hauling a giant red hose. Oh, so that's what they'd meant when they asked me about ooze! It was all making sense as they shoved the hose into my hands.

"Do I get to spray anybody I want?" I asked. A few minutes ago I would have automatically soaked Ashlynn, but of course she'd just helped me with my question. Alas, poor timing.

"You are going to ooze our mystery guest!" Stewart jumped around wildly. "That's right, we have the mystery guest inside the mystery box, and you, Emma, get to spray him with Ooze!"

Some people wheeled a large box onto the stage.

"When I say 'ooze,'" Stewart instructed me, "you point the hose at our mystery guest! And our mystery guest will be soaked in squishy, wet, brainy ooze!"

The audience yelled *"Ewwwww!"* It did sound disgusting. I wondered who I was going to be soaking with ooze. I got the hose ready and aimed it at the box.

"One, two, three . . ."

The audience counted along. . . . "OOZE!"

Gooey, squishy, oozy slime sprayed out of the hose and the mystery guest jumped out of the box. I got one look at the mystery guest and I almost fell over.

Enrique Rico!

"AHHHHHH!" the audience screamed.

"AHHHHHH!" I screamed too. Enrique Rico, the movie star—who also was taking graduate classes at a prestigious college, I might add—was standing in front of me onstage!

I saw his beautiful face, his notoriously thick and shiny hair for one glorious split second and then . . . I oozed him. Ooze went all over his hair and dripped down his face and all over him.

"I'm so sorry!" I gasped, but my mic had been turned off so nobody heard me.

"I've been OOZED!" Enrique yelled. He dripped brownish-gray ooze as he ran to the front of the stage and posed like a muscle man, and the audience went crazy. He slapped a couple of people's hands in the front row and sprayed stray ooze on them.

Then he ran up to me and high-fived me, too.

"Don't forget to go to my new movie, *Ocean Pirate Five*!" he yelled to the camera. Then he headed offstage, leaving a trail of ooze.

I realized I was still standing there holding the hose.

"I bet you weren't expecting that mystery guest, eh, Emma?" Stewart said as some guy ran over and took the hose out of my hands.

"No," I squeaked. "No, I was not."

"Okay, time for a question," Stewart said. "Emma, are you ready?"

No. No, I was not. *Come back, Enrique! I'll ooze you anytime!* The crew member pried the hose out of my clenched hands as I stood there, still in shock.

"I think we have stunned our contestant!" Stewart laughed. "You never do know what surprises await on *Brainy Mania*, do you? But now, it's time. If you answer three more questions correctly, you will be the Big Brain!"

I snapped back into competition mode. I was ready. Ask away.

"Next question, showing your brain: 'What is two-fifths divided by three-fifteenths? It's a hard one!" Stewart called out.

Oh, please. Mathletes basic. I quickly flipped the second fraction to its reciprocal and answered: "Two!"

"CORRECT!" Stewart and the audience went wild. *Now, this is the kind of entertainment business I'd like to be in,* I realized. The entertaining competition of smarts. Not that acting wasn't challenging for the brain, because it sure was. I could tell Payton absolutely loved acting, being someone else and trying on different personas. But it wasn't my thing. However, standing up onstage getting questions right while people cheered for me? Including Enrique Rico?

Oh, yes.

I tuned back in to what Stewart was saying.

 227

"Your prize is one more HelpLine. This time you can choose to call someone from your home."

I had already given them a couple names of people at home before I was onstage. They were going to call and see who was around.

"Who are you going to choose to call?" Stewart asked. The monitor that was facing me started to blink, and a crew member was pointing at a name so I would know who was home. I grinned when I saw who it was going to be.

"I want to call my friend Ox."

And suddenly Ox's face was being shown on all of the huge screens. Giant Ox—or should I say Oxen—were everywhere. I heard a couple of girls in the audience say, "Ooh." I frowned. That was *my* man. No oohing.

"Hi, Emma." Ox smiled at me. "I miss you."

Now the whole audience went *"Awwwww."* And that totally flustered me. Did Ox just say he missed me on national television? Hee hee hee hee. Oh my! Hee hee hee.

"I have your question ready," Stewart said.

Get a grip, Emma. I looked away from Ox and focused on Stewart.

"And the question is: What is the name of the stadium that is the home of the Los Angeles baseball team?"

"Emma, are you thinking what I'm thinking? Dodger Stadium?" Ox asked.

No, I'm thinking, What luck that my boy-more-than-friend knows his sports.

"Yes. Our answer is Dodger Stadium," I said confidently.

"That's right! And you win a prize for that answer!" Stewart said and the audience cheered. "It's a year's supply of Soyweiners! That's right, soy hot dogs with the taste that makes you feel like you're at the World Serics!"

Soyweiners? Okay, then!

"Thank you, Ox!" Stewart said.

"Thanks, Ox!" I said. Ox's face disappeared from the screen.

"Now for this next question, you get no help from anyone," Stewart said. "This is all you, Emma."

And then he asked me a question. It wasn't math. It wasn't geography, literature, history, or even fashion-related.

"Who was the last winner of *America's Top SuperPop Star*?"

What? I had no idea. I felt like that one time I was in the spelling bee and the announcer mispronounced the word so I was standing there, clueless. (However, that worked out just fine because they disqualified the announcer and gave me a new word.) (I won.) But this time . . .

I knew Payton would know this answer. She was probably down there, bursting. *Payton,* I called out through twin telepathy. *What is the answer?* And my twin telepathy told me . . . nothing.

"We need an answer! Who was the winner?" Stewart nudged me. "Five . . . four . . . three . . . two . . ."

"Um, Dustin Weaver?" I blurted out. Did I just say *Dustin Weaver?* I *knew* it wasn't Dustin Weaver.

The crowd groaned. Red lights flashed all around me. *Wrong! Wrong!*

The light flashed over the audience and I could see the look on Payton's face. She was thinking: *Duh, Emma, it's not Dustin Weaver!*

Oh sure, *now* my twin telepathy worked.

"Sorry, Emma! The answer is Masha Natasha!" Stewart groaned.

I prepared to be escorted off the stage in shame. I had lost. I could feel my shoulders start the slump but I put on my best game face, the one that I'd practiced at home. Only nobody was escorting me off the stage. Huh?

"And now it's time to . . . MEET YOUR DOOM!" Stewart yelled cheerfully. Cheerfully?

Wait a minute, why was the audience cheering? And not just the polite applause, like, *Oh well, you lost.* They were going absolutely insane, cheering and pointing . . . Behind me?

Stewart spun me around to look. I turned around to see that the curtain had lifted to reveal an enormous, giant, two-story . . . slide. Not just a straight up-and-down slide like on the playground, but one of those twisty slides that you see at a water park. And at the very bottom of it was what looked like a shallow pool.

It must be for the next segment of the game show, I decided. They chose me for the trivia segment for obvious reasons, and they probably chose someone else for the daring, enormous slide portion.

But that's when it got bizarre. I could hear the audience chanting my name. And Stewart walked me over to the giant slide and pointed to a set of steps that went up, up, up . . .

"Emma, are you ready for the Brainy Mania Doom Zoom Flume of Ooze?" Stewart asked me.

"Me?" I squeaked.

"You lose, you ooze!" he yelled, and motioned for me to climb up the steps.

No, no! I lose and leave! I opened my mouth to protest, but the audience started chanting.

"Ooze, Emma! Ooze, Emma! Ooze, Emma!"

It was actually kind of catchy. You never knew what was going to happen to you in Hollywood, did you? I had no choice. I began to climb. With each step the crowd chanted: "Ooze, Emma! Ooze, Emma!" The crew at the top gave me instructions to cross my arms and lie back and then . . .

Stewart led the audience in a countdown.

"Three!" I sat down the way I was supposed to. I peered down and tried to see what was in store for me.

"Two!" The first curve looked like it would be no problem as it was only a twenty-degree sloping obtuse angle. But I could see the start of the second curve, which looked like more of a challenge. Acute angle! Dangerous geometry ahead!

"One!" Everyone was yelling: "GO EMMA!"

And I went! I was lying on my back, zipping around the curves. Geometry flew out of my head as I picked up speed, winding down and around. Ha! This was fun!

"Wheeee!" I yelled, and I started to yell *"Woo-hoo!"* when suddenly—

Splat! What the heck? *Splat! Splat splat!* I was being oozed! Squishy, slippery ooze started squirting out of the sides of the slide! I felt it soaking through my pants and then my tank top and my hair. The whole backside of me was going to be soaked with ooze!

I had to admit this was pretty hilarious, and as I slid around another curve I laughed. Which turned out to be a bit of a mistake, in hindsight, because on the next curve the ooze dumped from above. All over my face!

I was so slippery I slid faster and faster while sputtering brownish-gray ooze. It tasted a little bit like chocolate pudding. Not too bad.

Then I realized that all of this was being filmed on television, so I tried to do it with a dazzling smile. And that's what I had on my face when I came to the end of the slide and was shot out of the chute. Then Newton's laws of motion came into play as I hit an outside force—a giant tub of ooze. Splashdown!!!! I sputtered and sat up. I raised my hands in victory.

And then a final blast of ooze sprayed me from a hose.

I flopped back, soaking in the moment. And soaking

up the ooze. If this was what losing felt like . . . I was LOVING IT!

"Ewww!" The audience was screaming with delight as I stood up, dripping goo. I bowed and waved, and when Stewart came over I flung some ooze on him.

Twenty-five

IN A GLAMOROUS WHITE CONVERTIBLE

After a crazy day of filming commercials and game shows, Emma and I were exhausted.

"I'm thinking we order room service and I hole up in the man cave," Dad said. But when we got out of the studio, something extremely strange happened.

"This is where we say good-bye," Zoe said to us. "Bye, Ash."

"Bye, Ashlynn," Emma and I said. I wasn't sad to see her go, but she'd had a few moments.

"Maybe I'll see you at camp," I said.

"I'll be sick of this skirt by then," Ashlynn said. "It's worth making my bed, don't you think?"

I reminded myself to have my parents request a different cabin from hers for me.

"Zoe, it's been awesome meeting you," I said as she gave me a big hug.

"Keep your enthusiasm," she told me. "And I look forward to seeing you in the commercial—and who knows what else someday?"

We walked out to the curb and saw . . .

A man in a chauffeur's uniform standing in front of a white convertible and holding a sign that said PAYTON WEAVER.

Zoe and my dad burst out laughing.

"Who's Payton Weaver?" I asked.

"That's you," Zoe said. "A publicist friend of mine tracked you down through me because her client wanted to get in touch with you."

"Payton?" The chauffeur handed me a large envelope. I was totally confused as I opened it up.

I read it out loud.

"'Sorry about the paparazzi and romance rumors. Please accept my personal apologies, an evening on the town, and a basket of highly sought-after exclusive items from the forthcoming Dustin Weaver merchandise collection.'"

I gasped as I read the final line. "'From Dustin Weaver.'"

"Enjoy," Zoe said. "When I told Dustin's publicist it was your first time in town, she thought you would like a tour."

"In a convertible?" I clapped my hands. "This is even better than a double-decker bus!"

"Who needs a man cave?" My dad said. "This is a guy's car."

He and the driver started discussing horsepower and blah blah blah car stuff. I looked over and saw Ashlynn standing there, looking jealous.

"Sorry you can't come, but . . ." I reached into the backseat of the car and spotted something perfect. I picked up a shrink-wrapped black T-shirt that had the words MRS. DUSTIN WEAVER on it. I tossed it to Ashlynn. "Finally I have some clothes from an exclusive collection before it's in the stores that I can give to you," I said.

Ashlynn laughed.

"Don't expect me to hand this down to you." She held the T-shirt close.

"Girls, are you ready to roll?" Dad was sitting in the front passenger seat.

Emma and I raced to the car and didn't even open the

doors. We leapt right into the backseat. Emma's jump was a little short and fell on her face, but fortunately the Dustin Weaver pillow and soft blanket with sleeves—both with his face printed all over—broke her fall.

"It can get a little windy with the top down," the driver said. "Dustin set you up with some supplies."

He handed my dad a baseball hat (that said I ♥ DUSTIN), and Emma and me colorful scarves (the tags read: FROM THE DUSTIN WEAVER COLLECTION). I took the bright pink one and Emma took the blue. We wrapped them around our heads in a glamorous style.

"Mine matches my shirt very nicely, don't you think? Turquoise and red are still in style this year," Emma said. Emma was wearing a red T-shirt that had the *Brainy Mania* logo on it. They had given it to her along with a white skirt after her clothes had gotten soaked with ooze.

"We have time to give you a little taste of the Hollywood side of our city," the driver told us. "I hope you enjoy the ride."

While he pulled out of the parking lot, Emma and I looked through the Dustin Weaver swag. There were posters, two more T-shirts, a bottle of *Dustin Weaver* perfume, Dustin Weaver nail polish, and a personally autographed picture.

Payton, it read, *I'll catch you when you fall.*

"Oh, that's so sweet," Emma said.

"Although slightly embarrassing," I added, remembering how I stumbled across the whole restaurant.

"I think I found the perfect souvenir for Tess." Emma held up a school supply kit plastered with Dustin's face. "There's even a higher-math calculator."

This was so cool. And speaking of cool, I felt a cool wind get stronger as the convertible turned onto a highway and picked up speed. I felt around in my tote bag and pulled out my white movie-star sunglasses. I slid them on and leaned back against the heated seats.

And I felt like a total movie star. I wondered if people driving by were looking at us and wondering who those fabulous twins were in the back of the gorgeous convertible.

Emma and I took pictures of each other.

"We are entering Beverly Hills," the driver said. The streets got wider, the flowers and trees got more beautiful, and the gates to the houses got higher.

"This is been the home of many stars, and the famous ZIP code 90210," the driver said.

"Just to warn you, my sister has a near-photographic memory for trivia," I warned the driver. "I'm sure she already knows every fact about Los Angeles."

"Not every fact," Emma said modestly. "I do know that Beverly Hills is actually a city in the county of Los Angeles—not part of the city of Los Angeles. The population of Beverly Hills is a little more than thirty-four thousand people. And look! We're turning onto Rodeo Drive. Payton, this is one of the most famous shopping streets in the world."

"Of course I know that," I said. "The most famous fashion designers have stores here. And did you know the most expensive store in the entire world is on Rodeo Drive? Even a pair of socks is fifty dollars."

"Remind me to never take your mother shopping at that store." Dad laughed.

"I wonder if someday I'll live around here." I sighed.

"I can see it now," Emma said. "You'll be a famous actress and your husband, Nick, will be a top director. Or maybe a guitarist in a band. You'll have a mansion in Beverly Hills and a beach house in Malibu."

"Can the beach house have a man cave for your dear old dad, who came all the way out here to chaperone you?" My dad turned around.

"Of course," I said.

"I don't think this trip was much of a hardship for

you, though," Emma said. "You've been spoiled. Are you going to want to go back home?"

"It's been a great vacation," Dad said. "But I miss your mother and I'm starting to get indigestion from that craft services table."

"Speaking of indigestion, is anybody hungry?" The driver pointed out the window. We had driven into a new area of town and we saw a line of people waiting on the street.

"Are they waiting to get into a show?" I asked.

"Believe it or not, they're waiting to get a hot dog," the driver said. "That's a famous hot dog place."

I couldn't believe people would wait in line that long for a hot dog.

"I am hungry," I admitted. "But I don't want to waste the night waiting for a hot dog."

"Do you like hamburgers?" the driver asked, and when we all said yes, he pulled up to another busy place. "This is a very famous burger and fries place," he said, getting out of the car, "but don't worry, I have connections. This is Dustin's favorite place, so they'll give me VIP service."

Sure enough, he was back in a few minutes with hamburgers, french fries, and sodas for all of us. We happily ate until the car pulled up in front of a place that looked familiar.

"It's the theater where the Academy Awards are filmed!" Emma said, jumping out of the car.

"It's the Hollywood Walk of Fame!" I said, following her and practically skipping along the street, looking at the names of famous people engraved into the stars on the ground.

"There are two thousand, four hundred stars embedded in the sidewalks," Emma said. We both pulled out our cameras and took pictures.

"Here's one for the munchkins in *The Wizard of Oz*." I pointed and took a picture for Sam.

"Here is one for another pair of twin celebrities," my dad said, looking down. "I'm sure you'll be more famous and successful than these two."

Dad was pointing at a star for Mary-Kate and Ashley Olsen.

"Sure, Dad." We laughed and then posed together for a picture.

"Say 'twin superstars'!" he said as he took it.

We saw a crowd of people milling around and went over to look. That's when I saw the famous area where stars put their handprints in cement.

242

And not just their handprints—some celebs put their footprints on their signatures, and one actor even put his nose in his star!

"There are more than two hundred concrete blocks," Emma said. "The first celebrities pressed their handprints in the 1920s."

"Look, Emma!" I pointed to where the actors from a wizard movie had pressed in their wands. Emma was looking at the *Star Wars* robot marks. Then we put our feet next to the shoeprints of actors and compared sizes.

I looked at all of the marks that actors and actresses had left in the cement. It was so exciting to think that Emma and I were actually here in Hollywood, and that for a brief period of time we were part of the entertainment industry too.

"Well I think this is as much excitement as my heart can take." My dad pretended to fan himself as he pointed to Marilyn Monroe's signature. "Plus, it's time to head back."

We climbed back into the convertible, and Emma and I retied our scarves.

"I'll take the scenic route," the driver said, and just a minute later we saw what he meant.

On the mountainside, not too far from where we were, was the giant famous sign:

HOLLYWOOD

"Originally, that sign said 'Hollywoodland' and was put up by a man to advertise his new housing development," Emma said. "They later took down the 'land' and the sign fell into disrepair. For years it read 'Hullywo d' because the letters were falling apart."

Now the sign was glowing brightly against the mountain:

HOLLYWOOD

"Dad!" I said. "Can you film this?"

"Of course," he said. He took my camera and held it up to capture Emma and me on video.

"Put on your sunglasses," I told Emma.

"Let me make sure I get the shot with the sign behind you," Dad said. "Say 'Shiny *and* shiny! Double the shiny!'"

"I never want to say that again," groaned Emma.

"Okay . . . Tween Twins, scene one, take one," Dad said. "And . . . action!"

Emma and I struck poses in the back of the convertible! We threw our hands up in the air and shouted, "Woo-hoo!"

"Mills Twins take on Hollywood!" I yelled, the wind whipping through my hair.

"Woo-hoo times two!"

Twenty-six

MIDDLE SCHOOL AUDITORIUM

"People! It's almost time! Please take a seat and settle down. We are in for a most exciting treat— the debut of our very own Gecko television stars!" Mrs. Burkle clapped her hands, the bracelets on her arms jingling wildly.

Today was the day that the commercial was supposed to air the first time! We'd gotten an e-mail letting us know that the commercial would air during one of the afternoon talk shows at 4 p.m. Eastern Standard Time (1 p.m. Pacific). And right smack in the middle of Payton's Drama Club and my mathletes meeting.

So Coach Babbitt and Mrs. Burkle had decided to bring our two groups together. Again.

"Go, Gecko mathletes!" someone yelled.

"Dramatic Geckos rock!" a couple of other people hollered back.

It was just like the bus trip down to New York City, where we chanted against each other. But then came together cheering each other on by the end of the trip.

"Real geckos rule the school!" Mason shouted from a corner of the room, where he sat with his twin brother, Jason.

"Uh, do you think he brought Mascot?" I whispered to Payton as we made our way toward the front of the auditorium.

"Let his mom worry about him," she whispered back. "You're off-duty."

"Counselor Case is here?" I asked and swiveled my head around. There she was—in a seat next to the principal. Oh boy, this could mean some good recommendations for college. Or bad ones. Depending on how our commercial turned out.

"I can't believe you haven't seen the commercial yet," Quinn said. I'd invited her to our "debut," even though she wasn't in mathletes or drama.

"No sneak previews. So be kind," I pleaded with her. She gave me a little side-hug of encouragement and then went off to talk to one of the drama girls.

"The twins have to get the front seats!" Cashmere yelled. She had been much, much nicer to us since we'd gotten back.

In the week since we'd returned from Hollywood, things had gotten back to normal pretty quickly. No more limos, no more celebrity sightings, no more giant slides filled with ooze. It was hard to believe that our trip had even happened.

Oh sure, everyone treated us like celebrities for the first couple of days. Sydney made Payton tell her every detail of the Hollywood "scene." Payton gave Cashmere one of the autographed Dustin pictures, which she promptly put up in her locker. I caught her blowing kisses at it.

I took a seat in the front row. Payton sat down next to me. Soon Tess arrived and sat right behind my sister.

"Hi, Tess!" I waved. Tess said a happy "hi" back. I noticed her autographed Dustin Weaver pin on her backpack and detected the faint scent of Dustin's perfume coming from her direction. Payton had hooked her up with swag too.

Somebody sat down next to me.

"Really Jazmine?" Payton said. 'You really think this seat is saved for you?"

"It's front and center." She sniffed. "I always sit front and center, with Hector by my side. Hector!" she stood up and waved her arms wildly.

"Her nonverbal communication is extreme," I said to Payton. "Do I look like that when I wave? I hope not. She's like a human pinwheel. Anyway, Jazmine, it's fine, you can stay. Just move down one. Then you can have a close-up view of me dominating the television."

Ha!

Jazmine frowned but scooched down one seat. She was wearing a gray T-shirt that said OH GEE! IT'S OUR SCHOOL'S GEOBEE WINNER! with a picture of an insane-looking bee holding up a globe. Even I thought it was bizarre-looking. So, I didn't get to beat her and wear that shirt. I was almost—*almost*—relieved.

"Besides, Jazmine," I said, "That's not really the front row. This is."

I slid down onto the floor, just as Ox sat down in the empty seat behind me. And I leaned back against his legs.

"Hey," Ox said, smiling down at me.

"Hi," I said, smiling back.

I caught a glimpse of Payton's face. I didn't need twin ESP to know she was thinking something like

Eee! Emma is leaning against Ox's legs!!! In public!!! Where everyone can see!!!

Time for her to focus on *her* guy. Up onstage, Nick was wheeling a large TV toward the center.

"I'm nervous," Payton whispered, leaning down to me.

"You're nervous now?" I whispered back. "You weren't nervous when we actually filmed the commercial, *or* when you filmed extra parts— if you know what I mean."

"Or," I said louder, "when you attacked Dustin Weaver."

"Did you say Dustin Weaver? He's so cute!" Jazmine unexpectedly butted in, and also unexpectedly sighed.

"Yes, we met him," I said. "You missed all that, huh? About how Dustin and Payton were dating—"

"What?" Jazmine gasped. I looked up at Ox. He was trying not to smile but failing.

"Welcome, everyone!" Nick suddenly said from the stage. "We have about five minutes before airtime."

"All right people." Mrs. Burkle clapped. "I think it would be nice to have a Q&A with the twins at a future Drama Club meeting. It would be valuable to hear their experiences."

"Mrs. Burkle! Mrs. Burkle!" Cashmere raised her

hand. "You should have Sydney share her experiences too!"

I turned around and saw Sydney shaking her head at Cashmere.

"Oh! That reminds me! We have a special surprise for you all." Mrs. Burkle handed something to Nick and said, "It's an advance copy of Sydney's commercial!"

The auditorium grew very quiet.

"Um—that's okay," Sydney said. "You don't have to . . ."

Nick popped the DVD in and, using a remote, turned on the TV and dimmed the lights.

"Come to Phineas Fish's Tire Heaven!" a man appeared on the screen. And then there was Sydney on the TV!

Wearing a giant tire costume. You could barely see her face, the tire was so huge and round. She stood, frozen, as little kids dressed in angel wings and haloes were flitting around her.

"Fish's Tires!" the man said. "It's heaven on wheels!"

The word "Discount!" appeared over Sydney's face, and then the screen went blank.

The audience stayed very quiet.

"Sydney, you looked beautiful." Jason's voice echoed through the auditorium.

"Yes." Coach Babbitt coughed. "Very nice."

"Wonderful interpretation, Sydney!" Mrs. Burkle trilled. And we all clapped.

"I hope our commercial is a bit more professional," I whispered to Payton.

"And less embarrassing," Payton whispered back.

But there was no more time to worry. Nick changed the channel on the TV, we watched the end credits of the talk show, and then . . .

Commercial break! This was it!!!!

Twenty-seven

MIDDLE SCHOOL AUDITORIUM

Nick hopped off the stage, but not before giving me a thumbs-up.

The first commercial was for cheese.

"Not us!" Emma called out. Everyone shifted impatiently. And then . . .

Eeee!!!

There we were!

"Look! There's Payton," someone yelled. "Or is it Emma?"

I didn't answer (because it was Twin #1—that would be me in my greasy hair. Hey, if people wanted to *think* it was Emma . . .) Then everyone fell silent as we watched . . .

OUR TEEN SHEEN TWINS COMMERCIAL!

I flashed back to the moment when we first walked onto the set. It was so busy and exciting! I thought about the director, Lewis. The AD clapping the clapboard. Ashlynn glaring from the sides. (No, let's not think about that.) The hair stylist and makeup artist and the crew! It had all come down to our faces on the screen.

And Emma tossed me the shampoo bottle! And there I was, and my hair was shiny! And I was cartwheeling (as Twin #2!)! And Emma was giving a dazzling—yes, dazzling—smile!

"Shiny *and* shiny!" We gave our dazzling smiles. "Double the shiny!"

Yay! I started to clap, but then realized the commercial wasn't quite over yet. Suddenly Ashlynn's face was on the screen.

There she was, looking pretty with her hair styled and shiny. And suddenly, a greasy liquid was poured on her. She screwed up her face and sputtered as she was completely drenched.

The voice-over announcer spoke: "Don't let your hair be attacked by oil and grease. Use Teen Sheen shampoo."

Ashlynn's face filled the screen as she looked disgusted and very, very greasy.

The auditorium was silent for just a second. And then everybody started cracking up and applauding.

"You guys were awesome," Ox said. Everyone was congratulating us and telling us that we did a great job.

Mason and Jason walked over.

"Greasy! Shiny!" Mason said. "That was cool! Who was Twin Grease and who was Twin Shine?"

"Uh," Emma said, "Mason, thank you for getting that note to Ox."

"Yeah, buddy," Ox said. "Good job."

I looked at Emma like, *Really?*

Emma leaned over and whispered in my ear. "Mason drew a stick figure that was supposed to be me and wrote '911.' Ox found it in his locker, but by then I'd talked to him and everything was okay."

Mason was beaming proudly. Jason scowled, clearly not used to his twin getting the positive attention.

"Hey! When that girl got soaked in oil, that was hilarious!" Jason said, bringing the attention to him.

"That girl looked familiar," Mason said. "Even Mascot thinks so."

"I'll explain later," Emma told him, leaning *awaaaay* from Mason, who was holding his gecko out toward her.

And then the gecko took a flying leap onto Emma's hair.

"Mascot sure knows shiny hair, doesn't he?" Emma said, waiting patiently as Mason plucked the gecko out.

"And our hair sure is shiny since we got our year's supply of Teen Sheen shampoo," I said.

Emma and I said at the same time: "Shiny *and* shiny! Double the shiny!"

"Your hair does look shiny," Jazmine James said unexpectedly. "I may have to get some for my own television close-up."

"You're going to be on TV?" I asked her.

"Of course." She sniffed. "When I make the National Spelling Bee this year."

Emma got up off the floor and crossed her arms.

"I believe you mean when *I* make the National Spelling Bee," my twin said. "And win it."

Jazmine crossed *her* arms and stared back at Emma. A Spelling Bee standoff? A good time to walk over to . . .

"Nick!" I said as he appeared by my side.

"Great job, TV star." Nick smiled at me. I smiled back. "I thought the camera work was really cool, how they captured the light and the angles. You looked really pretty."

Squee!

"Thanks," I said. "The way you set up the TV was good too, the best angles and everything."

Nick laughed, which made me laugh back. I was happy to be home with my friends, but . . . I did miss Hollywood a little too.

My cell phone rang.

"It's after school hours," Nick said. "Go ahead, take it; it might be your mom or dad." Nick went over to talk to Tess.

I checked the caller's name. It was *not* my mom or dad. I answered it.

"Hi, Shira!" I said.

"Payton! I hope it's a good time to call, 'cause Jessica and I wanted to share some news with you and Emma!" Shira said.

"Emma!" I called and waved her over.

"That Jazmine James is d-i-a-b-o-l-i-c-a-l," Emma said, coming up to me.

"Shira's on the phone!" I told her. "Shira, I'm putting you on speaker."

"Hi, Emma!" Shira said. "Say hi, Jess."

"Hi," her sister muttered.

"We have great news!" Shira continued. "We've both been cast in a student film. Sure, it's a student movie, but you have to start somewhere. Good experience."

"That's awesome!" I cheered.

"Congratulations!" Emma yelled.

"I'm Girl in Line Number Eight!" Shira said.

"Who are you, Jessica?" I asked.

"Grnummanie," said Jessica.

"What?" Emma and I both said.

"Girl Number Nine," Jessica said more clearly. "I get to stand behind Shira."

"You're stars!" Emma said generously. "We'll be able to say we knew you before you were both famous!"

"Who's a star? Who's famous?" Sydney rushed over.

"Uh, Shira and Jessica," I said into the phone, "this is Sydney. Shira and Jessica are our friends from Hollywood."

"Really?" Sydney squealed. "What are you in? Where did you get your head shots done? Did you ever have to perform as—er—something silly, like a tire, on your way to stardom?"

"I think you want to talk to Jessica," we all heard Shira say, giggling. "Bye, Emma and Payton!"

"I agree," I said. "Sydney and Jessica should get along really well. Bye, Shira!"

Emma and I stood there while the two new "friends" exchanged info so they could chat later.

"So," Emma said as Sydney gave me back my phone,

"What did you think of our national commercial?"

Sydney looked at us for a moment.

"Meh," she said. "Not bad. But Jessica's going to give me an inside scoop on getting into the movie business. That's way bigger than commercials."

Sydney practically skipped away on her platform heels.

"Okay, that was seriously funny," I said.

"Students!" Coach Babbitt hollered. "Three minutes left until the late buses and parent pickup!"

"Three minutes!" Mrs. Burkle echoed.

"Come on, let's go say good-bye to everyone before we catch the bus," I said to Emma . . .

. . . who was just standing there, frowning.

"Emma?"

"Diabolical," my twin was muttering. "That's what she is."

"Let's go." I rolled my eyes and dragged Emma back to our friends. "You can tell me all about it on the bus ride home."

Nothing Emma could say would bring me down. We'd been in a commercial! I'd double-acted double-shiny!

And it was double awesome!

Twenty-eight

ON THE SCHOOL BUS

"That was so exciting!" Payton bounced up and down on the bus seat we were sharing. "I still can't believe we went to Hollywood and shot a commercial, and everyone got to see it and it was so good!"

"Jazmine James got my science fair project disqualified," I said. I was not bouncing. I was sulking.

"What?" Payton said. "Why?"

"She saw me practicing my lip-reading skills with Jason," I said. "And she told Coach Babbit that I could use lip-reading to spy on other people during competitions. She said I could use it to cheat!"

"Oh, Emma," my twin said. "That's too bad. You would never cheat."

"Of course not." I frowned. "So I said, 'Due to ethical considerations and an erroneous attack on my integrity, I will withdraw my submission.'"

"Who did you say that to?" Payton asked, looking at me funny.

"Just Coach Babbitt and Jazmine James," I told her. "And Jason and Mason and Ox and maybe a few other people. Tomorrow I will repeat the announcement in science class. Maybe I'll add some quotes from scientists who, like me, have been unfairly charged . . ."

"Emma!" Payton said.

"Like Galileo," I said passionately. "And—"

"Emma!" Payton said. "Shhh!"

I shushed. No use getting riled up on a bus.

"So I need another science topic," I concluded.

"The homecoming dance is next week," Payton said, completely changing the subject. "Nick is doing the lights for the decorating committee and said the auditorium will be totally transformed into an Autumn wonderland."

"Wonderful," I said. "I can't wait." Actually, I could wait. I'd never been to a dance, I couldn't even dance, and I wouldn't know how to act around Ox at a dance. Everything about the dance intimidated me.

"So what color dress are you getting when Mom takes up shopping this weekend?" Payton asked.

Okay. This part didn't intimidate me.

"I was thinking a jewel tone—maybe emerald green or sapphire blue," I said.

"I'm going to wear blue," Payton said. "So you can't."

"Hey," I protested, "you can't steal my signature color! I get first dibs."

"Just because it's your signature color doesn't mean I can't wear it," said my twin. "You're saying I can't wear blue ever again and you can't wear pink?"

"I don't even like pink," I informed her. "But you're right. I can't ban you from blue."

We were quiet for a moment.

"How about you wear blue and I'll wear a floral print?" I asked. "That way no one will mix us up, yet we won't clash."

"Sounds perfect." Payton smiled. "We can be identical, but with our own individual styles. Ox and you! Nick and me! Major *squee*!"

"Y'know," I thought aloud, "perhaps my science fair project could be about identical twins."

"Um, no thanks." My twin rolled her eyes. "I don't want to be dissected or experimented on."

"It would be the *behavioral* branch of science." I shook my head. "Like I'd really dissect you. Ha ha. Wait! I have an idea!"

Payton looked at me suspiciously.

"I could study the effects of twin switching!" I exclaimed. "I could write up our previous experiences and analyze the outcomes."

"Don't get us in any more trouble," Payton warned. "This sounds like trouble, Emma."

"Of course we'd have to perform some experiments in different conditions," I continued.

"You want us to trade faces for science?" Payton shrieked.

"And clothes and personalities," I reminded her. "Hmm . . . The Effects of E = P and P = E: How the environment impacts genetically identical subjects."

"You are crazy," Payton pronounced.

"Crazy brilliant," I retorted. "Well, think about it."

"I'd rather think about our trip," my sister said. "Remember the convertible ride down Rodeo Drive? And the stars on the Walk of Fame? And the commercial shoot?"

"Of course I remember," Emma said, starting to smile.

"I have an infinite loop of 'Shiny *and* shiny! Double the shiny!' playing in my head."

"We rocked that commercial." Payton sighed happily.

"How about a science experiment about hair hygiene?" I said. "I'll use Teen Sheen shampoo and you can rock your greasy look—and observe how people respond to identical twins with different hair."

"Are you kidding me?" Payton said, outraged. "I am not going to have greasy hair!"

I burst out laughing.

"I was joking." I snorted. "Gotcha!"

The bus pulled up to our house. Payton and I grabbed our backpacks and headed up the aisle.

"We have fifty-two bottles of Teen Sheen shampoo," I said, "We'll never be greasy again."

We got off the bus and started walking up the driveway.

"Twinky swear?" Payton asked. We stopped.

"No more grease," I agreed. We locked pinkies and shook.

"You know," my twin said, "we've never gotten around to making a twinky promise about—"

"Don't say it," I interrupted. I knew Payton was going to say "twin switches." We kept putting off promising not to switch places again. We knew we should, but . . . some disaster always seemed to occur, and by switching, we'd manage to avoid it. And help each other out.

But trading places had also brought us plenty of trouble. Still, we could never bring ourselves to twinky swear. Because that meant forever.

"Emma! Payton!" Our mother came running out the front door.

For now, though, I was just happy to be Emma. And judging from the smile on Payton's face (nonverbal communication clue), my TV-star twin was happy to be herself too.

"Girls!" Mom squealed. "I saw the commercial! It was wonderful! I'm so proud of you both!"

"Thanks, Mom," we said.

"Just one question," Mom said. "Emma, when did you learn to cartwheel?"

Payton looked at me and we both started cracking up. Even our own mother couldn't tell us apart sometimes.

"Twins rule!" Payton said.

"Twins rule!" I agreed.

And we did our special hand-clap-slap. Hollywood was exciting, but it was good to be home.

Read on for more twin-tastic adventures
with Payton and Emma in . . .

TRIPLE
TROUBLE

*by Julia DeVillers &
Jennifer Roy*

Payton

One

autumn dance!
TICKETS ON SALE NOW!

I stared at the poster hanging on the wall in the hallway near my homeroom. My first middle school dance! So exciting! So scary! Exciting! Scary! *Yay! Eek! Yay!*

I was excited because I mean, Yay! My very first dance! So yay! But also eek!

The eek part was that it was our first school dance *and* I was going with a date. Yes, Nick had asked me to the dance! My first dance! My first date! My mom said okay since we were going all together in a group with our other friends. But Nick would be my date.

My first dance! My first date! What would we talk about? Could Nick dance? Would we slow dance? What if we slow danced and my hands got sweaty?

"Miss Mills," a voice called out, "will you be joining us?"

It was my homeroom teacher, Mrs. "Bad Breath" Galbreath.

Bad breath. I hadn't even thought of that. Oh no! What if I was slow dancing with Nick and I had bad breath? What if—

I snapped out of it. I guess I should be focusing on *What if Mrs. Galbreath gives me detention for being late?* I had an iffy history of getting in trouble in middle school, so I raced to the classroom.

"Sorry!" I said weakly as I slid under Mrs. Galbreath's arm while she was shutting the door.

Whew! Made it.

I slid into a seat near the back and set my tote bag down on the floor next to me. I scrounged around for my social studies homework. I felt my brush and mini-mirror. My papaya-flavored lip gloss (that I'd bought in Hollywood). Sunglasses (that I'd worn in Hollywood. I didn't need them here). I really needed to clean out my tote bag.

And there it was: my social studies binder. I pulled it out and put it on my desk.

I'd promised my parents that missing school for HOLLYWOOD wouldn't interfere with my schoolwork. Sigh. Hollywood was over. No more starring in commercials, being on TV game shows, taking glamorous convertible rides, or bumping into celebrities and having my name linked to them. No more being famous. But lots more social studies.

And if I didn't keep my grades up, there would be "consequences." My parents had already once "limited my after-school activities" because of my grades. They just started letting me participate in drama club *and* VOGS (our middle school's video broadcast show) again. If I didn't get my schoolwork caught up, they might take those away again.

Or the punishment could be worse! What if they grounded me? Oh no! They wouldn't ground me from the *dance*, would they?

Don't panic, Payton, I told myself. I would focus on my schoolwork and let nothing distract me. Question 1. What are the three export products of the country of . . .

I struggled to remember the answer from the chapter I'd read last night. There were times I wished I had Emma's brain. My twin sister, Emma, could read a textbook and remember practically all the answers not just the next day, but for the rest of her life. Emma would have no problem making up her schoolwork from the days we missed.

Emma would never get grounded because of her grades. *She* would never get grounded from her very first middle school dance.

Oh yes! Emma was going to the dance too! Emma had a date too. Ox had asked her to the dance. He'd asked me yesterday what color Emma's dress was so he could get her a matching corsage. Emma's dress was so pretty. Her fashion had definitely improved this year. She'd picked out a white dress that had purple flowers all over it. My dress was a jewel-toned sapphire blue. Even though blue was Emma's signature color, I'd seen it and knew one of us would have to wear it. Emma didn't like it, so it became mine, mine, mine.

Okay, enough thinking about the dance. No more distractions, Payton. What are the three export products of the country of . . .

The door to study hall opened, and a guy I'd never

seen before walked in. He had straight black hair that flopped a little over his face. He was wearing an olive-colored shirt, skinny jeans, and skater shoes.

I wasn't the only one distracted. Everyone turned to look at him.

"You must be our new student," Mrs. Galbreath said. "Welcome. Take any empty seat."

The guy didn't seem bothered when everyone looked at him. He walked my way and sat down in the empty seat right behind me.

"Please return to your studies, students," Mrs. Galbreath said so everyone would stop checking out the new guy. I returned my attention to my homework. Okay. Three export products of . . .

"Psst." The new guy tapped my shoulder.

I turned around.

"It *is* you," he said. "I thought so."

Oh! I'd been recognized. He must have seen our TV commercial and knew who I was. I felt so famous!

"Hi," I whispered, smiling a nice friendly smile so he'd know I wasn't a stuck-up celebrity and I hadn't let fame go to my head. Then I stopped smiling when I saw Galbreath looking at me. I turned back around.

Three export products of . . .

Poke, poke. The guy was poking my back again.

"Hey," the guy whispered. "Can you do me a favor?"

He slid a piece of paper toward me.

Oh! Oooh! He must want my autograph! Blush. You can take the girl out of Hollywood, but you can't take the Hollywood out of the girl! Hee hee.

I took the paper from him and wrote my signature across the back of the paper:

Payton Mills ★

I reached over and dropped the paper back on his desk. Then I turned around and faced my social studies homework. Such was the life of a tween star. Trying to balance Hollywood and homework.

"Psst." The new guy tapped my shoulder again. Yeesh, how do Hollywood celebrities ever get their homework done? I checked to see if Galbreath was watching us. She was, but she nodded at me to help the new guy. I turned around.

"You didn't do it," he whispered.

Confused, I pointed to my signature. I was even more confused when the guy flipped over the paper to the other side.

"No, I need you to do the math problems." He lowered his voice and looked around. "See? I'm new, and I have to take some placement test to see what math class I'll be in."

What?

"Someone said you were a math genius," he whispered. "So, can you just write the answers in there? You can miss a couple to make it more authentic."

Ohhh. He thought I was my twin sister. And he thought I—meaning Emma—would help him cheat. Um, no.

"Sorry, I'm not a math genius," I whispered back. "That's my twin. She's the math genius in the family."

"Oh, you've got one of those too?" He nodded. "So do I. But wait, are you any good at math at all? Can you just do this anyway? I hate math."

"Um, isn't a placement test supposed to help you get in the right math class?" I asked.

"Whatever," he said. "I have family pressure to get in advanced classes."

"Well, if it makes you feel any better, I know the feeling," I said. "Although my family is used to it. My sister is four grades ahead of me in math. And we're even identical twins! That's why you mixed us up."

Yes, sometimes even I almost mix us up. Like one time in a clothes store I went over and started talking to her. But then I realized it was a full-length mirror.

But there are differences!

I'm PAYTON, the twin who
- is one inch taller.
- has slightly greener eyes.
- definitely without a doubt has shinier hair—today, at least.

Today Emma definitely was not shiny, shiny, double the shiny. This morning she'd put her unwashed hair in a scrunchie. A green scrunchie! Fortunately, I'd had an extra rubber band in my tote bag and convinced her to change it. Otherwise, she would embarrass us. Yes, us. When you're an identical twin, there's always the chance that people will think your twin is you.

And I didn't want anyone thinking I'd wear a green scrunchie. Emma had to represent the Mills Twins better.

Sometimes being a twin could be annoying. Being *Emma's twin* could be seriously annoying. Like sibling rivalry times two. She's been cranky. And not very well dressed. I know she's been feeling stressed, but we were just in a shampoo commercial, representing good hair, yet she had put her hair up in a scrunchie?

Like I told her before homeroom: Represent the Mills Twins, Emma. Represent.

DOUBLE TROUBLE JUST TOOK ON A WHOLE new meaning....

TRADING faces

take two

times SQUARED

DOUBLE FEATURE

MEET BRITTANY, CASSIE, AND ISABEL. THREE GIRLS WITH BIG DREAMS AND BIG AMBITIONS.

Sometimes the drama during the commercials is better than what happens during the show. And sometimes the drama making the commercial is even better. . . .

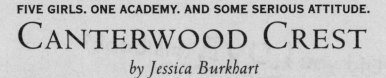

FIVE GIRLS. ONE ACADEMY. AND SOME SERIOUS ATTITUDE.

CANTERWOOD CREST

by Jessica Burkhart

HOME SWEET DRAMA
BOOK 8

CITY SECRETS
BOOK 9

ELITE AMBITION
BOOK 10

SCANDALS, RUMORS, LIES
BOOK 11

UNFRIENDLY COMPETITION
BOOK 12

CHOSEN: SUPER SPECIAL

INITIATION
BOOK 13

POPULAR
BOOK 14

COMEBACK
BOOK 15

MASQUERADE
BOOK 16

Don't forget to check out the website for downloadables, quizzes, author vlogs, and more!

www.canterwoodcrest.com

EBOOK EDITIONS ALSO AVAILABLE

Real life. Real you.

Don't miss
any of these
terrific
Aladdin M!X
books.

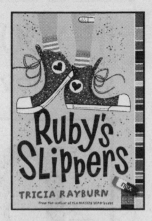